THE DRIFTER

JEREMY GERNHAELDER

◆ FriesenPress

One Printers Way
Altona, MB R0G 0B0
Canada

www.friesenpress.com

Copyright © 2022 by Jeremy Gernhaelder
Anick Côté, Illustrator
First Edition — 2022

All rights reserved.

No part of this publication may be reproduced in any form, or by any means, electronic or mechanical, including photocopying, recording, or any information browsing, storage, or retrieval system, without permission in writing from FriesenPress.

ISBN
978-1-03-913156-9 (Hardcover)
978-1-03-913155-2 (Paperback)
978-1-03-913157-6 (eBook)

1. *Fiction, Thrillers, Suspense*

Distributed to the trade by The Ingram Book Company

Dedicated to my father, Perry Gernhaelder,
a man who would do anything to make sure
that we always had clean clothes, a warm meal,
and a safe place to sleep.

Dear Billy,

I scarcely know where to begin this letter. To be honest, it is one that I hoped I would never need to write. However, given recent circumstances, I fear that my remaining time on Earth is now limited. Despite my fears, I still hold out hope that you may never need to read these words. If I am successful in stopping him, this letter will be nothing more than a journey for me into a past that I have long since buried. However, should I be the one to die, I would like you to hear the truth in my own words. At the very least, I owe you that much.

CHAPTER 1

October 4, 2011

The wind howled, and the rain pelted Kerry's coat as he hurried back toward his truck. The old man cursed himself under his breath as he finally emerged from the forest. Lily Chow had said on the radio that morning that the weather was going to take a nasty turn, but Kerry Giles had chosen to go out hunting anyway. Although the storms of October were fierce, he simply could not pass up the opportunity to get out into the woods on the opening weekend of bear season. Since Kerry had retired to Traders' Point nearly a decade ago, bears were the only type of game in the area that had eluded his rifle. Hunting may have cost him his marriage, but it was what he lived for.

Through the downpour, Kerry could just make out the shape of his truck amidst the darkness on the other side of the clearing. The rain had been coming down hard for nearly an hour though, and the ground in the clearing had turned to mud. Thankful that he had chosen to bring his waders with him, Kerry navigated his slender, seventy-one-year-old frame through the slick mess hidden beneath the tall grass. Fortunately, a life of putting up apartment buildings combined with a love of hunting and hiking had hardened his muscles for life, making the task far less of a challenge for him than it would be for an inexperienced man.

After nearly a dozen minutes of struggle, Kerry arrived at his truck. He opened the back door and tossed in his rifle and hunting gear. Then he pulled out a large towel and walked over to the front door. He laid the towel over the driver's seat, carefully tucking it in to make sure he minimized the amount of mud that would get on its interior, and then hopped in. Kerry started the truck and felt relieved as the warmth of the heater kicked in. Reaching into the glovebox, Kerry pulled out a small flask and took a swig of the spirit contained within. He was always careful not to overdo it when driving, but the internal warmth of the liquid was just what he needed to complete his self-rejuvenation before making the difficult journey back to town.

Although he had installed stacked tires on his truck, Kerry knew it would not be much longer before the trails became washed out, and he would be forced to camp out overnight in his truck. Such a prospect did not appeal to Kerry, for whom camping was the least pleasurable part of the hunt. Still, if he tried to take things too quickly, he'd be certain to slide off the road and into a tree, so he pulled the truck out of its spot and slowly navigated his way back toward the main road. The journey through the forest trails took the better part of an hour, and Kerry nearly got stuck a couple of times, but he finally managed to emerge back onto the paved road.

He sighed with relief and reached over to turn on the radio. During this momentary lapse of attention, Kerry swerved slightly and nearly struck a man walking along the side of the road. Seeing him at the last second, Kerry spun the wheel hard in the opposite direction, narrowly avoiding spinning out, and slammed on the brakes a few yards later. He took a moment to catch his breath. Then he put the truck into park and hopped out to see if the person was alright.

The man had dived into the brush on the side of the road to avoid being hit. As Kerry shone his flashlight in the man's direction as he slowly pulled himself to his feet and climbed back up to the road. He easily stood a head and shoulders above Kerry.

"Are you alright?" Kerry hollered over the storm.

"Fine," came the gruff reply.

"What are you doing out in this mess?"

"Just a bit lost is all."

Then the man began to walk off in the opposite direction of town. Even if Kerry had not almost just killed the fellow, he would not have been able to square letting him wander off into the storm alone with his Lord. Kerry rushed to catch up with the man.

"There isn't anything in that direction for quite a long way, buddy," Kerry. "Let me give you a ride to town."

The man looked toward the truck and then up at the sky and nodded with a sigh. Kerry pulled an extra towel out of the back seat of his truck and handed it to the man.

He wrapped it around his shoulders, and they both got into the truck. Kerry cranked the heat up and started off toward town.

After a few minutes of listening to the radio, Kerry became overwhelmed by curiosity. "So, what do I call you?"

"Drifter," he replied, eyes locked on the road ahead. "Drifter will do."

"Okay, Drifter. Nice to meet you. My name is Kerry." When the man did not reply or shake his offered hand, Kerry lowered it awkwardly. "Where were you headed?"

"Nowhere in particular," the man replied, pulling a stick out of his thick beard, his eyes still on the road.

"Ever been to Traders' Point?" Kerry asked cheerfully.

"No."

Puzzled by this response, Kerry pressed on. "Well, are you coming from somewhere nearby?"

"No."

Kerry wasn't sure if the coldness of the man's replies were because he'd nearly run him over or if this was just his guest's normal demeanour, but he could take a hint. Perhaps he was simply the kind of man who preferred silence. Based on his appearance and his answers so far, Kerry figured he likely wasn't a very social fellow. Kerry just hoped that the man wasn't the type to sue. They drove for several minutes with the only disruption of the discomforting silence being the songs on the radio. Then the drifter spoke up, causing Kerry to jump in his seat slightly.

"I'm looking for somebody," he declared. "Ever heard of anybody with the last name Heis?"

"Can't say that I have. Is the person a friend of yours?"

"Stop the truck."

"What?" Kerry asked with a laugh.

"You can let me out," the drifter replied sternly. "There's nothing for me here."

Kerry weighed his options. The drifter was clearly a man whom one should not mess with. However, Kerry thought that maybe he had suffered a concussion from the accident, and Kerry would feel as guilty as hell if something happened to the man in the storm. Still, the drifter clearly was driven by some sort of mission to find this "Heis" person. Kerry had known men like this before. He wasn't sure if he could dissuade the drifter from pursuing it for a time, but Kerry felt obligated to try.

"I'm not going to be doing that, friend," Kerry stated cautiously. "Even if I hadn't almost hit you with my truck, I could not let you walk out into a storm like this. Now, I suggest you let me take you into town for a hot meal, and I'll fix you up with a bed for the night. After that, we can call things square, and you can continue on your way. Sound good?"

The man sighed with frustration but made no move to indicate that he was going to put up a fight. Kerry continued to drive toward town, humming along with the various tunes on the radio.

***

Jenny Maysure smiled as milkshake shot forth from the nose of the man she loved. When he finished coughing, he glared at her. "Why must you do that?" he asked.

"I don't know what you mean, darling," she replied, feigning innocence.

Larry Hirsh shook his head and chuckled. "Your jokes are going to kill me one of these days."

"Well, at least you'll die happy!" she quipped, bringing on another bout of laughter from Larry.

As if on cue, the jolly, plump owner of the Diner arrived at their booth with their burgers and fries. Dianne Smythe had been running the town's only restaurant for as long as either of them could remember. The place probably looked exactly as it had when she took it over in the late 1980s, and Jenny had serious doubts that the previous owner had done any remodelling either. The place looked like an iconic diner out of the 1950s. Dianne set down the plates in front of them and then gave Larry a stern stare.

"Just make sure you don't spit up on my floor, kiddo," she said, ruffling his hair. "or else you'll be ending this date with my mop instead of a pretty girl." With a serious expression, she gestured at the gleaming white tile floor and then at the mop leaning in the corner. Larry pretended to be horrified, and they all had a good laugh. Then Dianne walked back over to the lunch counter to pour the only other patron, a visiting hunter, a fresh cup of coffee.

Larry grabbed the ketchup as if it were life-saving medicine and poured an ample amount over his fries. Jenny sighed and shook her head before taking a bite of her barbeque bacon cheddar burger. The savoury flavours danced across her tongue and began to settle the grumble of a belly that had skipped lunch for work. Larry was equally engaged in his meal, probably because neither he nor his father could cook well. They both ate in a pleasant silence.

At least that was the case until the drifter walked in. In a scene that felt as if it were out of a movie, lightning struck, thunder boomed, and the wind bellowed as the massive man stepped into the Diner. His hair and beard were long, graying, and scraggly. His eyes were dark and cold. He was taller than anybody that Jenny had met in her lifetime, and she suspected he had the frame of a man who had been hardened by many years on the road. His clothing, which was in tatters and soaked in mud, certainly reflected this. Kerry Giles squeezed by the man, who stood as still as a statue and waved to Dianne, who looked mortified.

"Evening, Ms. Smythe," Kerry said sheepishly. "Apologies for the state of our clothing."

"I suppose you got caught in the storm," Dianne replied with a sigh, gesturing for them to take a seat at the opposite end of the counter. She set down two cups and filled them with coffee.

Kerry moved forward to take the seat that was offered, but the large man remained where he stood. At first, Jenny thought that the man was staring at her, and, feeling intimidated, she ducked down into her seat. However, as the man continued to remain firmly in his place, Jenny realized he was actually staring past her toward Larry. Of course, Larry remained oblivious to this, his focus having returned to his meal the moment he saw Kerry. A wave of fear coursed through Jenny as she waited for what felt like an eternity before Larry finally noticed that she had stopped eating.

With a mouthful of burger, he looked toward the giant figure. "Do I have something on my face buddy?" he muttered mockingly.

The moment the words left her fiancé's mouth, the man rushed over to their booth and grabbed Larry's shirt. Before Jenny could do anything, the man pulled Larry out of the booth and shoved him up against the wall. "Heis?" he shouted. "Is your name Heis?"

"What the hell are you talking about?" Larry replied, now gripped by the same fear that Jenny felt. "Get this freak off me, Kerry!"

Kerry and the other patron in the Diner each took hold of one of the man's massive arms. "Let him go," Kerry said softly. "He's not the guy you're looking for."

The drifter looked over at Kerry and then back to Larry. "What's your last name?"

Larry looked too frightened to answer. Jenny stood up, fear replaced by fury. "His name isn't Heis! It's Larry Hirsch!" Seeing his puzzled expression, Jenny nodded, lowering her voice. "Please let him go."

Jenny's pleading seemed to snap the drifter out of his rage. He set Larry back down on his feet and muttered an apology before taking a seat at the counter as if nothing had happened. Kerry, looking extremely embarrassed, apologized several times to Larry and Jenny before joining the drifter. Although there was still concern on her face, Dianne moved over to the two men to take their order. The other patron shook Larry's hand and returned to his place as well. One look at Larry was enough to tell her that he was not willing to let this go. She embraced him.

"It's not worth it, love," Jenny whispered in his ear.

Larry looked at her face and sighed. "Alright, but let's get this food to go."

Jenny winked at him. "My thoughts exactly," she said, giving him a kiss.

***

Hank Lawson muttered a series of curses under his breath as the rapid knocking on his front door continued. He and his wife had gone to bed over an hour ago, and he intended to give this visitor a piece of his mind for waking them up. He secured the belt of his robe and rushed down the stairs. Then he turned on the porch light and threw open the door. The words "What the hell is the matter with you?" were already beginning to leave his lips when he caught sight of the behemoth standing before him.

"Sorry to bother you so late," said Kerry, whom Hank had not noticed until then. "but I was wondering if you might have something available for the night."

"I'll be staying for a while," the large man said gruffly to the surprise of both men.

Hank gave the man a skeptical look. "Have you got any money, Mister?"

The man stuffed one of his large hands into the pocket of his ripped coat and pulled out a fist full of soaked $50 bills. He pushed the pile into Hank's chest, nearly causing the elderly man to fall over. "Is this enough?" the man asked hoarsely.

Hank saw that Kerry was just as shocked as he was by the man's immense wealth. Hank took two of the bills and handed the rest back to the man. "I'm afraid the only lodge I have left has a cracked window, but you're welcome to take some wood from the pile and start yourself a fire."

"Won't be necessary," the drifter replied, taking the key from Hank. "I just ask for my privacy."

"As you wish, sir," Hank stuttered.

The huge man nodded, shook both of their hands, then walked off toward the lodge.

Hank gave Kerry a skeptical look once he felt the man was out of earshot. "Who the hell is that, Kerry?"

Kerry's expression was pleading in response. "Just take care of the guy, okay? I nearly hit him out in the woods tonight, and I really can't afford to have him sue me."

Hank sighed. "You owe me some game for this."

Kerry grinned. "Rabbit or venison?"

I guess I should start with our names. I am Robert Heis, and your mother and I named you Billy after her grandfather. My childhood was very different from the one you had. I grew up in a small city far away from here. I was the son of a factory owner, and it was always my father's plan that I would be the fourth generation to run Heis Footwear. He was a strict man and my lessons on how to be a "Heis" began at a very early age. When I did not meet his expectations, I learned from his strap to do better next time. At the time of your birth, I was already in charge of shipments and was soon to be promoted to VP of the company. Were it not for the tragedy that changed our lives, you would surely have followed the same path that I did. In some ways, I'm glad things worked out differently for you. You had a freedom in your youth that I never knew.

CHAPTER 2

October 5, 2011

When the bell at the front door chimed early the next morning, Dianne was in the kitchen preparing the trays of sugars, jams, and peanut butter for the morning rush. "Have a seat, honey," she called out cheerily. "and I'll be with you in a minute!"

When she emerged into the dining area, however, her demeanour changed instantly. Before her stood the drifter from the previous evening. The morning light cast his massive shadow over her, sending a chill through her body. Remembering the danger that he had posed to Larry Hirsch the previous evening, Dianne was far from comfortable with the idea of being alone in the room with this man.

"Kennedy!" she shouted toward the kitchen. "Get out here please!"

"Can't you just call me 'Ken'?" her son complained as he stepped into the dining area.

Seeing the large man in the doorway, Kennedy's muscles instantly tensed up. Even though he was shorter than the drifter, Dianne was certain that he would not let any harm come to them. He had been in the army, after all, and he knew how to defend himself. Still, the last thing she wanted was for a fight to break out in her home.

Fortunately, the drifter seemed to understand the implications and raised his hands in surrender. "I'm not here for a fight."

"So, what can I do for you then?" Dianne asked cautiously.

He pulled a stack of bills from his pocket. "I was hoping for some breakfast."

Dianne had never seen so much money before. She and Kennedy exchanged a wary glance and then she gestured for the man to take a seat at the counter. She put a hand on her son's shoulder, and he relaxed. "I'll be in the kitchen if you need me," he said loudly enough for the drifter to hear.

Feeling somewhat relieved that things weren't going to escalate to violence, Dianne walked around to the other side of the counter to pour a cup of coffee for the large man.

"I'm sorry for last night," the drifter said as she set the cup in front of him.

Dianne smiled. "Well. we all make mistakes, darling. I certainly have no right to pass judgement." Seeing his smile, she continued. "What were you interested in having?"

"A short stack of pancakes, five pieces of bacon, three pieces of ham, and a half dozen scrambled eggs," the drifter answered.

Dianne raised an eyebrow in surprise. "Do you want toast with that?"

"I'll take a couple of slices of rye if you have it."

Dianne nodded and retreated to the kitchen to give the order to her son and then continue her prep work. As she wandered in and out of the kitchen, she took time to study the man seated at her counter. The silver colour of his hair and the large wrinkles on his face hinted at a man in the later stages of life, but he clearly had not lost any of his strength. She gauged him to be twice the weight of her boy and suspected that, given the tightness of his garb, his body was likely chiseled. She also noted that he was a man of little expression and even fewer words. During the twenty minutes that it took Kennedy to prepare the drifter's order, the man did not say anything to her or the other customers who began to stroll in. When she set the food in front of him, he muttered a word of thanks and then dove in. Dianne poured him another coffee and then lost interest in the drifter as the rush began to pick up. In fact, she was so engrossed in serving her other customers, that she did not notice when the drifter rose to leave. When she returned to his place to see if he needed anything else, all that remained was a set of empty plates and two $50 bills taped to a short note of apology that he had tucked under his empty mug.

***

"Is this really the best idea that you've got?" Jenny's boss asked, emerging from his luxurious office into the large space they referred to as the newsroom.

"Come on, Cody," Jenny pressed. "You and I both know that this could be a real scoop."

"A stranger in town during hunting season is a scoop now?" Cody Barrens asked with a skeptical eyebrow raised. "Just how boring of a community do you think we are?"

"Don't downplay this, boss," Jenny countered. "A large stranger, who clearly isn't a hunter, comes into town and throws Larry against a wall in the Diner. How is that not news?"

Lily Chow emerged from her booth. "Sounds to me like she just wants to find out who put down her boyfriend."

Cody's girth shook as he laughed at the comment. Sometimes Jenny wondered if her boss kept them both employed simply because he enjoyed the friction that existed between them. Jenny blushed at the implication, but she refused to be deterred.

"Fiancé," Jenny sneered at the retreating radio host. "and you're just worried I might end up doing your husband's job for him."

That comment made Cody roar even louder with laughter. Jenny knew the old man could be swayed to take her side. She just needed to pull the right strings.

"What about the fact that he mistook Larry for this 'Heis' guy?" she asked.

Cody scratched at the short curls of his white beard and then shrugged. "People make mistakes."

"I'm telling you, boss, give me a chance on this, and you won't regret it. Have I ever steered you wrong?"

"Fair point, Jennifer," Cody reluctantly admitted. "But this is Barrens' Media, and that means I'm the one who gets to call the shots around here."

Jenny was on the verge of begging. "Just give me today, two days tops. I'll run this 'Heis' name through our archives and reach out to my sources."

"Well, . . ." Cody was wavering, and Jenny knew she had him where she wanted him.

"Trust me, boss," she declared confidently. "This could be the story that puts Barrens' Media on the map."

Before he could say anything more, she turned on her heel and darted out of the newsroom.

As she made her way down to the basement, Jenny had to admit to herself that she really did need to know what had possessed the drifter to attack her lover. Still, she was sure there was a genuine story here, and she was determined to see it through. Although she knew it would take her the bulk of the day to comb through all of the historical archives looking for "Heis," as the paper dated back more than a century, Jenny was sure it would be worth it.

***

A loud series of bangs shook the front door of Kerry's tiny cottage. Checking the clock on the wall, he noted that his guest was right on time. He turned down the oven and walked over to greet the drifter.

"Good evening," the man said flatly.

"Welcome," Kerry replied cheerfully. "I hope you had an enjoyable first day in town."

"Stayed in bed," the drifter declared and then smiled slightly. "The Diner makes good eggs."

Kerry was pleased by this. "So, you took my advice and made amends with Ms. Smythe?"

The drifter nodded, and Kerry stepped aside to let him enter. The drifter stepped into the well-lit room but made no further move. Kerry, who had turned back to his dinner preparations, failed to notice his guest's discomfort at first. When he did register it, he felt incredibly embarrassed. "Please let me take your coat," he said hurriedly. "and why don't you take a seat in the chair by the fire."

The drifter said nothing but did as he was asked. Kerry began to feel self-conscious, wondering if his modest little home was beneath a man who carried thousands of dollars in his pockets. He poured the drifter a stiff drink and took it over to him.

"I know the place isn't much," Kerry began awkwardly.

"It's perfect," the drifter muttered.

He took the offered glass from Kerry, drained it in a single swig, and handed it back.

"Well, I hope you like rabbit stew," Kerry replied, returning to the kitchen.

The drifter didn't acknowledge this comment. Instead he chose to silently stare into the small fireplace in front of where he sat. Kerry wanted to press his guest for more information but opted to focus on putting the finishing touches on the meal instead. He stirred the stew and checked the bread. Then Kerry set two places at the table, each with a bowl, a plate, a glass, and a large spoon. A few minutes later, the two were seated before steaming bowls of stew, massive slices of garlic toast, and tall glasses of beer. For several minutes they enjoyed the meal in silence.

When the drifter spoke up, Kerry nearly choked in surprise on a mouthful of toast.

"Been here long?"

Kerry took a swig of his drink before responding. "About eight years now."

The drifter nodded and took a drink of his own. "How's the hunting?"

"The game here is good," Kerry replied, gesturing at the food. "and plentiful. Are you thinking about taking up the sport?"

The drifter dipped his toast into the stew and took a bite. "Perhaps," was all he said in reply.

"Well, you won't be disappointed if you do," Kerry said, happy to finally have managed to engage in conversation with the man who still felt like a stranger to him.

"What about the trails?" the drifter asked, not looking up from his meal.

"There's plenty of them," Kerry replied with a smile. "You won't be likely to run into anybody else out there, if that's what you're worried about."

This seemed to please him. The drifter paused for a thoughtful moment and then continued with his questions. "How's the terrain?"

"The forest is pretty thick along the trails. It's mostly made up of spruce and birch trees as well as a variety of bushes, so it can be challenging to get a clear line of sight. That said, there are very few hills and valleys out there, so using the natural camouflage to your advantage is key. There are also several clearings scattered around Traders' Point that serve as good places to set up a blind. It can get pretty muddy out there when the storms roll through, but you can manage if you're careful about your footing," Kerry concluded with a grin.

The drifter nodded his approval and then returned to his meal. Kerry followed suit, glad to have made a bit of progress in earning the stranger's friendship.

***

Jenny stormed into her mom's small house through the back door and tossed her bag against the white and purple striped wall in frustration. The smell of roasted chicken was the first thing to greet her upon her return.

"Is that you, dear?" her mother called from the kitchen.

"Yeah, Mom!" Jenny shouted as Larry walked into the small space between the inner and outer doors that served as a mudroom.

"Rough day, sweetie?" he asked, giving her a kiss.

"That doesn't even begin to describe it," Jenny complained as they walked into the kitchen. "I had to practically beg my boss to let me look into this 'Heis' guy."

"You mean the massive freak who tried to beat me up last night?" Larry asked.

"What's all this now?" Jenny's mother asked, looking concerned.

"Last night a giant out of a horror movie came to town, Mrs. Maysure," Larry said before Jenny could respond. "and he wanted to kill me because he thought I was somebody else."

"It wasn't that bad, Mom," Jenny replied, trying to calm her mother's fears.

"You weren't the one he threw up against the wall," Larry shot back as he dropped into a wooden chair at the small round dining table.

Mary Maysure turned back to the early 1990s-model oven to check on the chicken. "I'm not so sure that you should be looking into such dangerous matters, dear."

"It's not like I'm running into a burning house to interview this guy at gunpoint, Mom," Jenny replied, glaring at Larry as she did so.

Larry shrugged and pretended to look innocent. Mary silently busied herself stirring the mashed potatoes, a tear rolling down her cheek. Jenny knew she had just messed up, but, although she wasn't in the mood to deal with her mother's concerns, she also knew she couldn't afford to worry her either. Ever since Jenny's father was killed a dozen years ago in a hunting accident, her mother had been on medication for anxiety and depression. She still managed to run her little herb and natural remedies shop, but she was a shell of the woman she had once been. Jenny walked over and put her arms around her mother.

"I'm sorry," Jenny said softly. "I promise that I was just looking into the name the guy mentioned, so I could write something for the paper. I didn't go anywhere near him, Mom. I ended up spending the whole day in the basement going through the archives."

"Did you find anything?" Larry asked, curious now.

"No," Jenny replied regretfully. "I checked as far back as forty years and couldn't find any mention of a family with the name of 'Heis' moving into or out of our area."

Mary looked pale for a moment but recovered quickly. "Perhaps that's for the best," she suggested.

Thinking of the smug look on Lily's face, Jenny shook her head. "No, I need to find out what this guy's story is."

"How do you plan on doing that?" Larry asked. "Are you just going to walk up to that freak and ask him why he decided to manhandle me?"

"Not me," Jenny replied with a smug grin. "Us."

My family was famous in the city where I grew up. It was established by three industrious families more than two centuries prior to your birth. The names of the founding families were Heis, Roth, and Morrison. They used their money to secure several thousand acres of farmland in order to create a railway to join the northern and southern parts of the country. Over time the descendants of these families had a hand in every business within the city limits and beyond. In doing so they established their power over everyone else who lived there.

To an outsider it would appear that my life was one of privilege and respect, as nobody would dare to cross my father in public. In reality, my childhood was one of scorn, jealousy, and rejection by the majority of my peers. They mocked me for my privilege and beat me whenever they had an opportunity to do so away from the watchful eyes of the adults. The irony is that if they had understood the pressure I was under at home, perhaps they might have realized that I was actually the one who was jealous of them. I envied their freedom to choose the life they wanted to live, to come and go as they pleased without having to answer to anyone. Most of all, I envied their anonymity. In a city of two thousand people, I hated to be so easily recognized. I just wanted to disappear.

CHAPTER 3

October 6, 2011

The sun rose into a fantastic array of purples, blues, oranges, and pinks while Hank and Sue Lawson drank their coffee in their rockers on the porch. It looked like it would be another fantastic day outside, and that meant another fantastic day for hunting. Despite the storms of the previous few days, they held out hope that hunting season would have good weather overall. Of course, good hunting meant good business for Hunters' Lodge. Hank smiled at the thought.

In the decades since they had won the lottery, neither Hank nor Sue had ever regretted their decision to move to Traders' Point. They had enjoyed hunting there in their early years, back when their current home was little more than a long log cabin, and visitors needed to camp in tents on the grounds when they visited. The Lawsons had purchased the place for a reasonable sum and acquired a significant portion of land around it to develop their travel destination. To date they had built ten small cabins for rent and a large ranch house for their own family. They had also managed to put all three of their children through university without taking out a single loan.

Their investment into the small community had paid off for everyone who lived there as well. In the last four decades, Traders' Point had doubled in size. Several new families had moved there to revitalize other businesses in the area or start their own. These families brought children and built small homes to settle in year 'round, leading to plans for a school and a library to be developed in the near future. Hank was certain that Sue would find a place working with the kids once that happened, as she had homeschooled their lot and the few others who lived there since the 1980s, and it would please her greatly. Although that would mean hiring additional help to maintain the place, Hank was happy to see his wife so excited again.

In truth though, the best part of living in Traders' Point was how much everyone there looked out for one another. Hank had spent his youth living in a city and hated every minute of it. The street crime kept him constantly looking over his shoulder. He had lived in a cramped apartment with his family, having to evade drug dealers every time he went out to play. His only escape had been the weekends that his father took the family into the forest to hunt. At the time, Hank did not realize how important those hunts were for his family's survival, as they could not always afford the prices at the market. He had simply enjoyed the freedom of not having to be around other people all the time. The quiet stillness of the woods brought peace to his soul.

Hank's thoughts were shattered when the drifter's shadow fell upon him. "Good day," the drifter said without much enthusiasm.

"Good day to you, sir," Sue replied sweetly. "I hope you're enjoying your stay with us so far."

"Yes," he replied, placing two more $50 bills in front of Hank. "I plan to stay a while longer."

"Delighted to hear it," Sue said, beaming. "Why don't I fetch you a mug of coffee?"

Before the hulk of a man could respond, she had darted into the safety of the house. The drifter stood rooted in place, staring toward the door she had entered. In the light of day, Hank realized he was just as uncomfortable having the man around as he had in the darkness of the night he arrived. The drifter's physical size and secretive nature were both a cause for concern. Hank feared that the longer he permitted the man to stay, the more likely it was that he would be inviting trouble to his door.

"You planning on doing some hunting?" Hank asked.

"Something like that," the drifter muttered.

"Well, I'll need to fill out some paperwork if you plan to stay longer," Hank said. "So, how's about you give me your name to start?"

The large man glared at him, and for several minutes, Hank was concerned that he was about to be pounded into the dirt. Even so, Hank refused to back down. Eventually, the drifter broke the stare and sighed.

"My name is Maverick Dunn," he stated bitterly before pulling out another $50 bill. "You had best keep that to yourself though."

Before Hank could respond to this threat, Sue returned with fresh coffee for the three of them. Not wanting to cause his wife concern, Hank pocketed the bills and ceased his interrogation. This seemed to please Dunn, who sipped his brew in silence. Unfortunately, Sue was not a woman to appreciate silence in social settings.

"Are you finding your way around Traders' Point well enough?" she asked.

"Yes," Dunn stated flatly.

"That's good." Sue smiled, not seeming to notice the man's dour demeanour. "Anything exciting planned for today?"

"Need supplies," Dunn answered, then narrowed his eyes in a hostile way toward Hank. "Going hunting soon."

"Oh, excellent," Sue replied, cheerfully unaware of the threat he posed.

Hank wished she would just let the man leave, but he knew better than to expect that from Sue. If he was curious about the man, she would be downright engrossed in solving every last bit of the mystery lingering about him. Despite his uneasiness in allowing her to continue, Hank did not wish to alarm his wife, so he held his tongue.

"So, why'd you pick Traders' Point to come to?" she asked.

"Had family in the area once," Dunn replied.

"Really? Anybody I would know?"

"Perhaps." Dunn's voice showed interest for the first time, unnerving Hank further. "Ever heard of the Heis family?"

"Can't say that I have," Sue replied with a briefly dampened spirit, but then she smiled. "But if they ever lived here, there will certainly be a record of it."

"Where could I find it?" Dunn asked.

Hank saw a chance to send him away and jumped on it. "Perhaps you could try the doctor in town or visit the radio station."

Hank was grateful when his tenant seemed to take the hint. Dunn nodded, set down his empty mug, and wandered off toward Main Street without saying another word to either of them.

"He seems like a nice fellow," Sue said as she took the mugs inside.

Hank wished he could be as optimistic as his wife.

***

Jenny made sure that she woke up an hour earlier than usual so that she could be standing in front of the police station with coffee when Sheriff Jay Chow arrived. The single-story, red-brick building seemed to glow in the morning sun behind her. Upon seeing his vehicle turn toward her, she silently prepared herself for the mission at hand. Everyone in town knew Jay had been promoted to sheriff two years prior because nobody else who was eligible to take the post was willing to travel to the middle of nowhere to take it. However, just because he was inexperienced did not mean that he couldn't be quick-witted at times. Jenny just hoped that his wife hadn't mentioned her story to him over dinner the previous evening. As Sheriff Chow descended from his pickup, she put on her most disarming smile and walked over to greet him.

"Good morning, Sheriff," she said cheerfully, extending the cup of coffee toward him.

"Good morning, Jenny," the thin man said and then sighed. "You know that my wife is trying to get me to cut back on caffeine, right?"

"You know it," Jenny replied with a wink.

Jay shook his head in defeat and took the Styrofoam cup. After a big swig of the warm brew, he smiled and opened the door to the building. Jenny followed him into the large office and waited for him to set his things down before she began.

"How was your night?" she asked sweetly.

"The youngest kept me up half the night," Jay grumbled. "Let's save the dance for today though, Jenny. Could you just tell me what you're after?"

Jenny secretly thanked whatever gods had given his son night terrors and got straight to the point. "I'm sure you've heard about the drifter who has come to town?"

"You mean the one who beat up Larry?" Jay chuckled. "Lily might have mentioned it to me."

Jenny blushed. "The guy practically assaulted my fiancé and—"

"Relax," Jay said, holding his hands up in defeat. "I meant no offense. Are you here to press charges on Larry's behalf then?"

"No," Jenny replied, shaking her head. "I don't think Larry wants that."

"So, what would you like me to do then?"

"Well, I just thought that, seeing as how you're the only law enforcement officer in town, that you might want to look into this guy."

The amusement fell from Jay's face. "Watch your step now," he warned.

Jenny regretted losing her patience. "I'm just looking for a little information here, Sheriff."

"Last time I checked, it wasn't my job to help you do yours," Jay stated through clenched teeth.

Jenny could see that she had lost her opportunity. She rose, picked up her own cup, and headed for the door. When she reached it, she turned back. "The guy isn't here to hunt game, Sheriff. He means business, and the longer he's here, the more likely it is that you're going to have a situation on your hands. I'll be sure to do my job then."

Before he could reply, she walked out the door. It seemed that if she wanted to get to the bottom of this, Jenny would need to go straight to the source.

***

Larry walked through the door that adjoined their family home to Hirsch General Store at half past nine that morning with his head hung low. He had slept through his alarm again and failed to meet his dad for the start of the business day. His dad was busy setting up the cash register when Larry entered the front room.

"Late again, Larry," his dad, Stan Hirsch, said, stating the obvious, as he did when he was irritated.

"Sorry, Dad," Larry said, walking over to the boxes his father had left by the shelves for him to stock.

"Perhaps you should stop staying out so late with your girlfriend," his father suggested.

"She's my fiancé," Larry corrected.

"Until you're wed, I need your focus to be here, son."

"I know. I'm sorry."

"With the season started now," Stan continued. "I can't keep up with the demand for supplies alone."

"I'll be on time tomorrow. I promise."

Stan sighed. "I'll go unpack the dairy order in the back."

Larry hated to disappoint his father. He often felt like he was unable to live up to his father's expectations. Though he did not know why, Larry always felt like there was a distance between him and his dad that he simply could not bridge. He had stayed to help run the business when the opportunity for post-secondary education presented itself, thinking that would show the man how much he loved him, but it only seemed to make things worse. Things had become incredibly tense between them once he and Jenny had announced their engagement, and Larry was looking forward to being wed so he could live with her family full time.

Larry was on his knees stocking the lowest shelf when the bell announced the arrival of their first customer.

"Dad, can you get that?" he hollered toward the back room.

When the bell sounded again, and his father failed to answer him, Larry stood up and walked to the front counter. Before him stood the giant man who had embarrassed him in front of Jenny two nights prior. Larry's skin burned with shame at the memory, and he clenched his fists.

"What are you doing here?" he demanded.

"Came to apologize," Dunn said with a detached voice. "And to buy some milk."

Larry wanted to shout at the man or strike him, but he knew that would only shame his father. Instead he told the man which aisle to look in for the milk and then walked around to the other side of the counter. He wondered where his dad had gone and why he wasn't there to serve the customer. His father was dedicated to his schedule, and Larry knew he wasn't meant to step out for a cigarette break until an hour from now.

Dunn grabbed a jug of milk, a block of cheese, a loaf of bread, and a box of Captain Crunch. Then he returned to the counter, and Larry began to ring up the items.

"You look very familiar," Dunn said, studying Larry's face.

"Yeah, I gathered that," Larry snapped. "Do you want a bag for these?"

"No," Dunn replied, his eyes on the sign above Larry's head. "Your family has owned the store for quite a while."

Though it wasn't a question, Larry felt obligated to reply. "It was opened by my Great-great Uncle Howard in the sixties."

"Lived here all your life then?"

Larry summoned his courage before he replied. "Look, I don't know who this 'Heis' guy is, but it's not me. My dad inherited this store in the eighties, and we've lived here ever since."

Dunn held out a $50 bill, which Larry took and then handed back his change. Without saying another word, Dunn grabbed his bag of groceries and walked out of the store. As soon as he was gone, Larry breathed a sigh of relief. Unnerved by the experience, he was trembling with fear. When he recovered a few moments later, Larry walked into the back room to find out why his father had not come out to serve the customer. Instead of his dad, Larry found a note attached to a crate of milk. It simply read, "Gone for coffee."

***

The soft knocking on his office door surprised Dr. Ike Sindell. Looking over at the grandfather clock that was his pride and joy, Ike noted that his final appointment had ended over twenty minutes ago. Concerned by the disruption to his evening routine, he shut and locked his desk drawer.

"Come in," he said.

His young assistant slipped in and closed the door behind her. She was clearly nervous about something, which only served to increase his own concern.

"I'm sorry to disturb you, Dr. Sindell," Brittany said timidly, "but another patient has just arrived and insists on seeing you."

"Who is it?" Ike asked, attempting to mask his own uneasiness.

"I'm not sure," she replied, refusing to look him in the eye. "I've never seen him before."

"Oh," Dr. Sindell said, adjusting his striped tie. "Well, does he have an emergency?"

"I was afraid to ask him, Uncle," Brittany said, tears starting to roll down her cheeks. "He just insists that he needs to speak with you before you leave today."

Ike walked over to her and pulled her into a hug. "It's okay, sweetie. I'll take care of him. Why don't you slip out the back door while I go to greet him?"

His niece looked at him with concern, but he simply kissed her on the forehead. "Go home to your mother. I'll see you tomorrow."

He escorted her out of his office and sent her down the hall to the back exit. Once the door closed behind her, he slipped on his white coat and went into the waiting room. Upon seeing him, the man rose to his feet, and Ike understood immediately why Brittany had been so nervous. The man would have towered over her, and the hand he extended toward Ike was likely the size of Brittany's head.

Ike swallowed and shook the man's hand. "How can I help you?" he asked.

"Looking for a relative. In need of a donor," the man replied with a deep and intimidating voice. "Goes by the name of Hirsch."

Ike's features reflected his confusion. "Do you mean the store owner?"

The man shook his head. "Not the current one. I'm looking for the former owner."

"I'm afraid he passed away some time ago."

"Any other descendants in the area?"

"No, sir," Ike said. "To be frank, I was surprised the former owner had any relatives at all."

The man stepped closer to Ike. "Why is that?"

Feeling intimidated, he stepped behind Brittany's desk before responding. "The man was a loner. As I recall, he came out here in the early sixties and built the store. He never married and I'm not aware of any relatives visiting him prior to his great nephew arriving about a year before his death."

The giant man leaned over Brittany's desk and asked his next question in a tone that made Ike fear for his very life. "Ever heard of anybody with the last name of Heis?"

"I-I-I have never treated anybody by that name," Ike stammered. "I have only been practicing here for the past twenty years though. Perhaps you might find out more by visiting Barrens' Media. They've been around these parts for longer than any of us. If the person you're looking for has ever come through this town, they would have a record of it."

The man grunted and nodded in reply. Then he turned and walked out of the front door without saying another word. Ike rushed over to it and locked it as soon as he was certain the man was gone. Trembling, he returned to his office to seek out the bottle of spirits he would sip from before delivering bad news. Tonight he expected that it would take the remainder of the bottle for him to recover his composure.

By the time I was in grade ten, I had learned to accept my life for what it was and to embrace the possibilities it provided me. I was one of the top students in my class, a wide receiver on my high school football team, and the president of the student council. My father had even told me he was proud of me once. Deep down, however, I believed that my success was due to people's intimidation of my family's name rather than my actual abilities. I couldn't handle that. I became depressed and began to drink to cope. I would cut myself when I was left at home alone on my parents' social evenings. There were times that I considered ending it all rather than living this lie any longer.

It was then, when my self-esteem was at an all-time low, that your mother moved to the city. Her name was Marsha, and she was the most beautiful girl I had ever seen. Her father had lost his career and his savings along with it. As a result he had been forced to take a job as a custodian at my father's factory, and her family of four had to live in a one-bedroom apartment in the worst part of the city. The first time I saw her, I knew I needed to be with her. I was mesmerized by her beauty and the way she laughed in class whenever I told a joke. I wanted to spend time with her, and when we did, I fell even harder for her. She was the kindest person I had ever met, and I desperately wanted her to see me for the person I truly was. To see the person who existed beyond the name of Heis. I wanted to give her everything that she could ever ask for, including my heart, and I did.

CHAPTER 9

October 7, 2011

When Jenny arrived at Larry's place, she found his father standing outside. Mr. Hirsch had a stern look on his face as he smoked a cigarette. Based on the tiny pile of butts on the ground around him, she suspected that he had been up for a few hours. Though his eyes were closed, she was certain that he knew she was there.

"Good morning, Mr. Hirsch," Jenny said with all of the cheer she could muster.

Stan nodded but said nothing. Jenny stepped by him and entered the small four-room house. Hearing the door open, Larry walked into the kitchen/living area to greet her.

"How did you sleep, darling?" he asked and then leaned in to kiss her.

"Better than your father, I'd wager," Jenny replied quietly.

"Best not to go there," he stated in an equally quiet tone. "Hope you're hungry for pancakes," he added.

"Sounds great," Jenny lied.

She loved the man who stood before her, and she was glad that he wanted to show some initiative. Unfortunately, neither he nor his father could cook much of anything unless it came from a box with step-by-step instructions. She took a seat at the modest oak table and waited for him to finish preparing their meal. Stan walked into the house as Larry was setting the large platter in the middle of the table next to a variety of syrups.

"Morning, Dad," Larry said with a smile. "I hope you like the pancakes."

"Let's just get eating," Stan replied harshly. "The shelves won't stock themselves."

Seeing the disappointment on Larry's face, Jenny spoke up. "They look delicious. Could you please pass the corn syrup, honey?"

"Well, do you want corn or honey?" Larry asked, causing them both to break out laughing.

Stan said nothing. He merely spread butter over a small stack of pancakes and began to eat. Jenny looked at Larry, who shrugged and followed his father's lead. They ate in silence for several minutes. Jenny could feel the tension between father and son, and she was desperate to ease it.

"How's business, Mr. Hirsch?" she asked.

"Same as ever," he mumbled without looking up.

"Actually, something really interesting happened yesterday," Larry said, causing Stan and Jenny to pause to look at him.

"Do share," Jenny encouraged.

"Well, that drifter that you're so interested in came by the store to get some groceries."

Stan had frozen midway between taking a drink of his coffee, but Jenny was too eager to let that stop her. "Did he say anything more to you about this 'Heis' guy?"

"No, but he did apologize to me for what happened in the Diner the other night."

The shattering of Stan's mug made both of the lovers jump. Larry started to rise, but his father raised a hand.

"Don't bother!" he roared. "I'll clean it up. Just go next door and start setting up for the day."

Jenny glared at Larry. "I thought you said you could come with me to interview the drifter this morning."

"He can't!" Stan declared. "We have too much to do!"

Larry tried to stand by her side. "You said I could have a few hours today because you needed me to cover later for your doctor's appointment."

"Enough!" Stan shouted. "I'll not be told how to run my business by either of you. I told you to get to work, boy!"

Larry's body shrank in defeat, and he quickly left the room. The moment they heard him enter the store, Stan turned to Jenny. "It would be wise not to involve yourself in matters that don't concern you," he hissed.

Furious, and seeing that there was no point in further discussion, Jenny walked out the back door, making sure to slam it behind her. The more that fate seemed to stack the deck against her discovering the truth about the drifter, the more determined she was to find it out. Still, she had promised her mother that she would not try to interview the man on her own. Her search through the archives yielded nothing, she felt certain that Sheriff Chow wasn't going to help her, and now she could not go directly to the source.

Sadly, that meant she was left with only one other option. Jenny needed to make a phone call.

***

Brusard's Sporting Goods had been family owned and operated since it was built fifty years ago. It had been opened by their grandfather and run by their father and uncle before Arthur had officially taken it over five years ago. They weren't just known for having the best and most ample supply of hunting goods in the area though; their family were also famed hunters. Their uncle had even competed in sport shooting at the Olympics. The Brusard men knew the land like the back of their hands, and they offered their customers advice that never failed. It was a matter of family pride, which is why Arthur was so frustrated with the supplier who had him on hold. The season had barely begun, and their stock of rifle ammo was already beginning to run low. Arthur could not afford to have the shipment arrive late. When the person on the other line returned with the unfortunate news, Art slammed the phone down in frustration.

"No luck then?" John asked as he placed a few new pistols in the display case.

"Apparently, that big storm the other night washed out the road to the south. We won't be able to get any new stock in until the tenth," Arthur said with a groan.

"That bites," John agreed as he walked over to unlock the front door. "Although I suppose that also means we'll also have fewer customers to make purchases."

John always tried to look on the positive side of things. Arthur envied him for that ability. Of course, his eighteen-year-old brother was more interested in the stock than he was in maintaining the business as a whole, so he didn't need to think about the bigger picture. There were plenty of hunters, both local and travellers alike, in Traders' Point already, and when they learned that they would see little competition that weekend, they would surely rush to the store for extra supplies that they would be unable to provide. Arthur was so distraught that he did not realize his brother had ceased to move since he opened the store.

"Holy shit," John muttered as he took several steps backwards.

Arthur snapped out of his dismay and looked toward the front door. There he saw what had disturbed his brother. It was the large, burly frame of a man who had to duck to clear the doorframe as he stepped inside. The bulk of his muscular frame nearly filled the width of the doorway as well. Seeing the concern on his brother's face, Arthur stepped forward to greet the new customer.

"Good morning, sir. Is there anything that I can help you with today?"

"Need some gear," the man declared in a voice that matched his size.

John rushed back to the other side of the gun counter, ready to show the man anything that might interest him.

"Sure thing," Arthur replied, masking his impatience. "What's your interest, sir? We have the best in hunting and fishing supplies, so I'm sure we can accommodate you either way."

The large fellow seemed to ignore what Arthur said and walked past him. He stepped over to the back of the room and browsed the store's selection of traps. John shrugged at Arthur, who stood there looking perplexed. Arthur knew better than to upset the customer though, so he simply walked over to the cash register and waited for the man to complete his shopping. The man returned to the front with several snares meant to catch animals ranging in size from rabbit to deer and two large bear traps.

"Need a rifle," he grunted.

"Do you have a permit?" John asked nervously.

The man said nothing, electing instead to point to a weapon on the wall behind John. Seeing the fear in his brother's eyes, Arthur spoke up.

"I'm afraid that you need to show us some ID in order to purchase a weapon, sir."

The fury in the large man's eyes when he spun to face Arthur made the owner's knees shake. He reached under the counter and gripped the gun hidden there as the man approached him and slammed a license down on the counter.

"Satisfied?" he bellowed.

Arthur glanced at the name and photo before the man scooped it back up. He nodded to his brother. "Show him the weapon."

"Sure thing," John answered in a trembling voice. "This is one of our finest models."

The man took the gun and checked the sight and the chamber. Nodding with satisfaction, he pointed to a box of ammo, and John handed it to him. He took the gun and the ammo over to Arthur and then walked back over to John.

"Need a shotgun," the man stated. "And a pistol."

John glanced over at Arthur for approval before handing the guns and the corresponding ammo to the man as well. The massive man then brought them over to Arthur.

"Do you need anything else, sir?" Arthur asked.

"A knife," the man replied. "A large one."

Arthur retrieved a sheathed blade from beneath the counter. He handed it to the man, who removed the sheaf and inspected the blade. He replaced it, nodded, and handed it back. Arthur rang everything up and began to sweat when he saw the total. However, he seemed unfazed by it. He placed the sum upon the counter and picked up all of his purchases in a single bundle.

"What exactly are you hunting for, sir?" Arthur asked, no longer able to contain his curiosity.

He walked toward the door while uttering a single word of response.

"Revenge!"

***

As Jenny took a seat in the cramped space that served as her office at Barrens' Media, she couldn't help envying her only colleague. While Lily had enough space to house all of her radio equipment as well as two large desks and seating for four, the sides of Jenny's modest desk touched the walls of her office. She also needed to push her chair tight up to it in order to close her door when she left. Even still, being a reporter had been her dream ever since Jenny had first learned to read by flipping through the newspaper in her mother's shop, so she refused to complain or let anything stand in her way.

With that in mind, Jenny sighed before picking up the phone and dialing her cousin's number. It rang several times before a familiar voice answered.

"Agent Ferris, speaking," came the cheerful but professional response.

"Hi, Derek," Jenny said, biting her lower lip. "Have you got a minute?"

She imagined his lanky body leaning back in his chair and smiling as he replied. "Little Jenny Bean, is that you?"

"Derek, could you drop the silly nickname already?" she asked impatiently.

"Oh, I think you know I can't do that," he replied. "So, how are things in the sticks?"

"They're fine," Jenny said through clenched teeth and then took a deep breath. "I have something I need you to look into."

Derek groaned. "Not another hunter without a license, I hope."

"Not at all," Jenny replied. "This is serious."

"Okay. Lay it on me."

"We have a stranger in town. He's a huge guy, and he's definitely not a hunter. Although, to be honest, I don't know what he is."

"You think this stranger is going to be on the FBI's radar?" Derek asked, sounding surprised.

"Not sure," Jenny admitted, "but I know he's got a violent streak. He had every intention of breaking Larry's face over a simple case of mistaken identity."

Jenny heard Derek sigh and click his tongue. "So, this is about some guy beating up your boyfriend?"

"Fiancé," Jenny grumbled. "Will you just do this please?"

"Of course, Jenny Bean," Derek replied. "You got a name?"

"Heis," Jenny said, then looked up as she heard a loud discussion break out in the main office. "I need to go."

"You owe me some of your mom's herbal medicines for this," Derek replied as she hung up.

Opening her door a crack, Jenny was shocked to see the drifter standing in front of her boss. Cody looked as if he were about to lose control of his bladder as he stared up at the large man. The drifter's hands were balled into fists, and his face was beet red, so Jenny could understand why.

"I'm sorry, sir," Cody said cautiously. "As I told you already though, I'm not aware of anybody named 'Heis' moving into or out of this area."

"You haven't even checked your records!" the drifter yelled.

"My parents established this printing press more than eighty years ago," Cody replied with matching fury. "I know every story that we have ever run, and I do not know of anybody named Heis!"

If looks could kill, the drifter would have murdered her boss several times over. "What about the Hirsch family?"

"I'm afraid you have overstayed your welcome, sir. Now will you leave on your own, or should I call the sheriff?" Cody asked, unwilling to back down.

Even though Jenny was certain his eight-seven-year-old heart would give out before a punch could be thrown, she felt a certain pride at knowing that Cody was willing to stick up for the people of his community.

"This isn't over!" the drifter roared as he stormed out of the front door.

Cody turned to Jenny as she emerged from her office. "I want you to find out everything you can about that man!"

He walked into his office and slammed the door so hard that it shook the timber partitions that formed it.

***

Ike's stomach had been uneasy all day. The moment Brittany had informed him that he had an appointment with Stan Hirsch for his annual physical, he knew that things were going to get complicated. Ike had been plagued by nightmares of the giant who had visited his office the previous evening. The fact that the man had been so insistent upon learning about the Hirsch family had disturbed him greatly. Ike had seriously considered walking over to Stan's house that night to tell him what had happened, but he ultimately decided that he couldn't. Even though he had not examined the man, he had accepted him into his office under the condition of doctor-patient confidentiality.

Now that Ike was face to face with Stan though, it took everything he had not to say something. Fortunately, Stan was not one of his more talkative patients, so Ike was able to carry out the physical without much conversation.

Just when Ike thought that he was going to get through it without revealing his secret, his worst fears were realized.

"Something bothering you, Doc?" Stan asked as he buttoned up his shirt.

"No," Ike said, feeling sweat trickle down his forehead. "Why do you ask?"

Stan shrugged. "You just seem really quiet today. You didn't even ask me about my boy."

Ike panicked at Stan's words. "I'm terribly sorry. Is Larry doing okay?"

"He is," Stan said. "In fact, he told me something interesting this morning."

"What was that?"

"Apparently, a stranger has come to town."

Ike dropped Stan's medical file, papers scattering all over the floor. He bent down and scooped them up. "That's interesting," he muttered.

Stan handed Ike a few of the papers. "What's even more interesting is that he seems to have an interest in my family."

"Oh, really?" Ike took the papers with a trembling hand.

"In fact," Stan continued, "he even mistook my son for somebody named 'Heis' and tried to attack him."

Ike could not mask his fear any longer. "I'm sorry, Stan."

"You've seen him too, haven't you, Doc?"

Ike nodded. "He was here last night."

"What did he want?" Stan asked.

"H-he c-came in here to ask questions about your family history," Ike stammered. "But I didn't tell him anything."

"Of course not," Stan replied, putting a hand on his shoulder. "I know you wouldn't break the law."

"He also asked me about this 'Heis' person." Ike was overcome by his fear now. "Do you think we should tell the sheriff?"

"Don't involve him, Doc," Stan replied. "I'll deal with him myself."

My father never approved of my relationship with your mother, which only made me want to be with her even more. He declared that Marsha was trash, that her family was trash, and that my dating her would embarrass him in front of the other founding families. He forbade me from being with her, but even he was not powerful enough to prevent our love. We would steal moments together whenever we could, away from the prying eyes of his spies. We would go on picnics, walks in the woods, and find places to be intimate together. I even took my grandmother's ring from my mother's jewellery box to propose to her.

In time my father saw that I would not be reasoned with. He was surprised for the first time in my life when I told him that I was taking Marsha and leaving home if he would not give his approval. As I was his only heir, I knew he would never allow it. His response was equally shocking for me though. He had told his lawyers to prepare a contract for me to sign. It stated that he would approve of my match and even support our union financially provided that I went off to college on my own. My father expected me to earn top grades while I was there and to return to take my place in the company business. I signed without hesitation.

CHAPTER 5

October 8, 2011

Jenny had not been the only employee of Barrens' Media to hear the argument between the drifter and Cody the day before. Lily had been sure to go home and prod her husband, Jay, for every bit of knowledge that he had about the mysterious man as soon as her radio broadcast ended. Unfortunately for Jay, he had not taken an interest in the stranger. After all, during hunting season, the strangers in Traders' Point could outnumber the townsfolk at times, and the man had done nothing to put himself onto Jay's radar. This excuse had not gone over well with Lily, and a night on the couch had made certain that Jay knew it. So, when she told him the next morning that they needed milk for supper, he didn't hesitate to run over to Hirsch General Store the moment he was on break.

"Morning, Stan," he said, tipping his hat as he walked in.

"Morning, Sheriff," Stan replied from behind the counter.

Jay walked over toward the coolers and nearly knocked over Larry, who was carrying a box of goods to stock.

"Sorry, Sheriff," Larry said without looking up. "Didn't see you there."

"No harm done," Jay replied cheerfully.

Jay watched Larry dart around the corner of the aisle with his box and remembered what his wife said about the boy's run-in with the stranger. Thinking he might have a chance to redeem himself at home, Jay abandoned the milk and followed Larry.

"I hear you had a spot of trouble the other night," Jay said, surprising Larry so much that he dropped the can he was putting on the shelf.

"No, sir," Larry replied timidly. "No trouble."

"Now, son," Jay said, placing a hand on Larry's shoulder. "There's no shame in being assaulted by a larger man who got the jump on you."

"He didn't assault me," Larry protested. "Just threw me against the wall is all."

"Are you two talking about that huge beast of a man?" Arthur Brusard asked, rounding the corner with a box of cereal in hand.

"Morning, Arthur," Jay replied, trying to mask his frustration at the intrusion. "I suppose you've seen this fellow as well?"

Before Arthur could reply, Stan entered the aisle. "Go fetch us all some coffee, boy!"

Larry didn't need to be asked twice, running off like a rabbit that had managed to escape a predator. Jay was furious that he had missed his chance to probe Larry further for information, but perhaps he could still salvage something out of the situation.

"So, what were you saying about this 'beast,' Art?" he asked.

"This man, Maverick Dunn, came into my shop yesterday," Arthur replied with a chuckle. "Bought enough supplies to start his own war with all of the animals around here. Paid for it all in cash too."

"Really?" Jay asked in a tone that he used to encourage suspects to talk more.

Arthur nodded. "Bought several guns with plenty of ammo for each plus a large knife and even an assortment of traps for catching a variety of game."

"I don't like it, Sheriff," Stan said. "A man with that size and raw strength was a threat to begin with. Now that he's armed, we could be in serious jeopardy."

"You're just saying that because of what he did to your boy," Jay stated calmly.

"I'll put this 'beast' down if he attacks my son again!"

Jay was going to say something, but Arthur chimed in. "Any parent would do the same, Sheriff. If this guy came after my little girl, I'd shoot him dead between the eyes."

"Well, I can't be having the citizens of Traders' Point attacking the tourists," Jay said and then sighed. "I guess I'll have to have a word with this fellow. You said his name was Dunn?"

"Aye," Arthur confirmed. "Maverick Dunn."

Jay nodded and then excused himself before leaving the store. It would be several hours before he realized that he forgot to buy milk.

***

The phone was ringing off of the hook as Jenny ran into her office. She threw her things onto her desk, picked up the receiver, and slammed the door behind her.

"Hello?"

"Tsk, tsk Jenny Bean," Derek replied mockingly. "You'll never catch a scoop if you keep sleeping in."

Jenny rolled her eyes but chose to ignore his insult. "What have you got for me, Derek?"

"Straight to the point, huh?"

"Cut the crap," Jenny replied, "or I'll let your mom know that you're holding out on me."

"Fine," Derek said. "I was calling to tell you that I got a hit."

Jenny pumped her fist in triumph. "We're finally getting somewhere."

"This isn't a joke," Derek replied. "The guy you asked me to look into is serious trouble, Jenny."

"I can handle a guy with a few arrests for bar fights," Jenny scoffed.

"The guy is wanted for murder, Jenny!"

Jenny was stunned. She had expected that the guy would have a past, but this possibility had never crossed her mind. "Tell me what happened," she said, pen in hand.

"The man you described matches the description of a man named Maverick Dunn. Over two decades ago, he was accused of murdering his sister. They said he even cut up her body and tried to dispose of the pieces down the drain."

"That's sick."

"That's not even the worst part. It turns out that Dunn was actually framed. A whole bunch of the evidence was tampered with, and the principal witness in the crime later admitted to being paid off."

"So, Dunn is innocent then?"

"Don't jump the gun, Jenny Bean," Derek chided. "Or you'll miss the best part."

"Go on," Jenny said, tapping her pen impatiently on her desk.

"Well, it turns out that this 'Heis' guy—whose name was Albert Heis by the way—is the one who orchestrated the frame-up. Apparently, he was some rich fuck with a long family line, and he used his wealth to put the blame squarely at Dunn's feet."

"Why did he do that?"

"Nobody knows for certain. The cops speculated that he was covering up for his son, who was married to the sister at the time. However, before the matter could be investigated further, the son disappeared. Then the courts decided to release Dunn, and he decided to pay Albert a little visit."

"I'm guessing that visit didn't end well?"

"Dunn is suspected of beating the man to death over a several-hour period. Broke over a dozen bones in the guy's body. Then he supposedly raided the safe. Helped himself to more than one hundred thousand in untraceable bills. He hasn't been seen since."

"Wow," Jenny exclaimed.

It was more of a story than she could have ever hoped for. This could very well be the story that launched her career. The story could lead to better jobs in the city and a chance to be the sort of journalist that she had dreamed of being since she was a child. She needed to confront the drifter and find out if he really was Maverick Dunn. If so, perhaps she could be the one to break a cold case wide open and reveal what really happened.

"Jenny?" Derek asked with concern. "Are you still there?"

"Yes," she replied excitedly.

Derek sighed, knowing there would be no point in trying to talk her out of this. "Just promise me that you won't do anything stupid."

"I promise," Jenny lied.

***

Jay wasn't surprised to find Hank Lawson sitting in his rocker when he walked over to Hunters' Lodge.

"Evening, Hank," Jay said, tipping his hat.

"Evening, Sheriff," Hank replied between puffs on his pipe. "What brings you by?"

"I'm afraid there may be a spot of trouble with one of your guests."

"Is that so?" Hank replied with a skeptical look. "Are you planning on making an arrest?"

Knowing Hank's primary concern was his business, Jay tried to reassure him. "Nothing like that at this point. I'm just looking to have a conversation."

Hank looked at Jay thoughtfully for a minute, paused to inhale from his pipe, and then nodded his consent. "Who are you looking for?"

"Big fella. Wears a tattered coat and carries around a large stack of money."

Hank sighed. "You're looking for Dunn. You'll find him in the lodge at the edge of the property."

"Thanks for your cooperation," Jay said and then walked toward the lodge.

As he approached it, Jay was surprised that a man with the sort of cash to pay for everything outright would be willing to stay in such a place. Of all of the buildings on the property, the lodge was the smallest. It was also located the farthest from town and was clearly in need of repairs. Jay was about to knock on the rickety door when it was flung open with such force as to knock him over onto the ground. When the stranger saw the sheriff on the ground, he muttered an apology and extended a hand to help him up. Jay noted that the man had a strong grip to match his impressive size.

"Mr. Dunn, I presume," Jay said as he stood up.

Jay noted that the man looked visibly annoyed at the mention of his name, but he simply nodded. "Yes."

"I'm Sheriff Chow," Jay began, "and I have come to inquire about your business in Traders' Point."

The man said nothing, simply gathered the bundle of wood that he had come out to get in the first place and then returned inside. Not used to being ignored, Jay followed him inside.

"It seems there have been reports made about violent behaviour displayed by you, Mr. Dunn," he said, "as well as reports of you purchasing an assortment of firearms."

"Buying guns isn't illegal," Dunn grunted.

"True," Jay said, his confidence wavering slightly. "but my concern is regarding what you plan to use your guns for, Mr. Dunn."

"Hunting."

"Hunting what exactly?"

Dunn stared at Jay, who could tell Dunn was trying to intimidate him. Jay would have none of this though and just stared right back until the large man relented. Turning to look out the cracked window for a moment, he muttered something under his breath. Then he turned back to Jay. "I'll move on in the morning."

Jay nodded, satisfied by this response. "Well, alright then. I guess I'll leave you to your packing, sir."

He tipped his hat to the large man, who did not seem to acknowledge the gesture, and then headed toward his truck. Jay hoped this news would be enough to please his wife's need for a scoop.

Going away to college and leaving your mother behind was the hardest thing I had done up until that point in my life. Although your mother had begged me not to leave her, I knew this was the only way for us to be together. So, at my father's insistence, I attended the finest business school in the nation. He had paid for a private residence for me to live in under the sole condition that Marsha was never permitted to come there. Knowing that he would have ways of ensuring that I kept my word, I had to survive on letters from your mother and our time together during the vacations from my studies. My father felt that, if Marsha truly loved me, she would be able to wait for me to return in order for us to earn his approval for us to wed. Though it would be tough, I was determined to prove my father wrong and show him that our love was true. So, I worked harder than I ever had before, driven by my desire to return to your mother, and completed my studies two months ahead of schedule. I earned the highest grades I could and felt certain that my father would welcome me home as a success. I had proved myself both as a student and as a man dedicated to the woman I loved. I believed that all of my dreams were finally within my grasp.

CHAPTER 6

October 9, 2011

Jenny was determined to get the story behind her cousin's findings no matter what. Since Sheriff Chow wasn't going to help her, Jenny decided that she wasn't going to share what she had learned about Dunn so far until after she wrote her article. Unfortunately, since Larry's dad kept insisting that he needed help in the store, she would have to do things on her own.

The first step was to locate where Dunn was staying. Although the only place to stay in town was Hunters' Lodge, Jenny knew that Hank would never willingly permit her to go onto his property to conduct an interview. The last time he had, Jenny had written an exposé about the number of hunters coming to town with outdated permits, so she couldn't blame him. Of course, Jenny had spent her entire life hiking in the woods surrounding Traders' Point, so she was confident that she could approach any of the buildings on Hank's land without being noticed. However, if she picked the wrong building on her first try, she would surely be caught before she could make a second attempt. Fortunately, she had a plan for getting around this hurdle.

After dropping by the Diner to grab a couple of coffees to go, Jenny ran through the rain over to Kerry's place and knocked on the door.

He was slow to open the door and blushed upon seeing her standing there, soaked. "Oh my goodness, Jenny. Come in and get out of this storm."

"Thanks, Kerry," she said, stepping in and handing him the coffee. "I hope you don't mind me dropping by."

"Not at all," Kerry replied with a grin. "No sense in trying to go out hunting in this mess, so I've got nothing better to do today. What brings you by?"

"Well," Jenny began, launching into her carefully constructed lie, "I'm afraid I need your help."

"Really?" Kerry asked enthusiastically. "Is it for a story in the paper?"

"Exactly," she replied with a wink. "I'm thinking of writing a story about the fellow you brought into the Diner the other night. What did he say his name was?"

"Afraid I don't know his real name," Kerry replied. "He only asked me to call him 'Drifter.'"

"Oh, I see," Jenny said, pretending to be disappointed.

"I know where you can find him though," Kerry said, hoping to regain her favour.

He had played right into her hands. "That would be great Kerry," she said, smiling in encouragement.

"I took him over to Hunters' Lodge. I'm sure he won't be hard to find."

"You wouldn't happen to know which cabin he's in, would you?"

"Sure do," Kerry replied. "He took the building at the edge of the property."

"The one with the cracked window?"

"That's the one."

"This is perfect," Jenny said with a big smile. "You've been really helpful."

She must have laid it on a bit too thick though because a look of concern spread over Kerry's face. "You aren't planning on writing anything nasty about him, are you?"

"Of course not," Jenny said as she patted his hand. "I just want to give him a chance to share his life story."

Kerry's smile returned. "Well, I'm sure it will be a fascinating read."

"I guarantee it."

***

After leaving Kerry's place, Jenny ran into the office to update her boss and grab the materials she would need for her interview. Then she began the long hike through the woods to navigate around Hank's property to the last cabin. She was grateful that Dunn had chosen that building because it was the easiest to approach directly from the treeline. It took the better part of an hour to reach it. By then her clothes were soaked through and caked in mud, but she was confident that it would all be worth it. Still, Jenny paused for a moment, feeling ashamed about breaking her promise to her mother, but then she pressed on. She needed to know the story behind "Albert Heis" and how it related to her lover.

Jenny poked her head out of the bushes to see if the coast was clear. Then she crept up to the door and knocked. "Mr. Dunn?"

"He's gone!" an angry voice boomed from behind her.

Jenny turned to find Hank standing before her with a shotgun in hand. "Would you please put that down, Mr. Lawson?"

He lowered the gun. "What are you doing on my property, Miss Maysure?"

"I came to interview Mr. Dunn," Jenny replied. "Where is he?"

"The hell if I know," Hank said, then spat on the ground. "Sheriff dropped by and spoke to him last night. Perhaps you should check with him."

"You're lying!" Jenny shouted, though she knew better.

Hank's eyes burned with anger. "You dare to call me a liar on my own property?"

Jenny cursed her bad luck. "You must know something."

Hank shrugged. "Man was gone when I came down to check if he needed more wood this morning. His stuff is gone, and he's paid up, so I couldn't care less where he's at now."

"I don't suppose you'll let me take a look inside to see if he left anything behind to indicate where he was heading next?" she asked, struggling to contain her anger and disappointment.

"Not a chance," he replied, cracking a smile. "Now, are you going to walk off of my property on your own, or should I call the sheriff to escort you?"

Jenny stormed off toward the main road without another word.

***

The morning had been quiet, just the way Jay liked things in his community. He decided to take some time to polish the framed photographs on his desk. His fingers lingered over a snapshot of his great-grandparents, whom he thought fondly of. His great-grandfather had immigrated from China to find work in the days when mining and railroads were essential to America's development. Jay was proud of the man's legacy of hard work and hoped that he made his ancestor proud with his own dedication to his position as sheriff. He nearly knocked this frame off his desk when Jenny burst through the doors.

"How dare you!" she exclaimed.

Although he was shorter than her, Jay stood with the confidence of a man twice his size. "What's your problem?"

"I came to you in confidence for help with a source!" Jenny stated furiously. "Not to help you kick him out of Traders' Point!"

"Ah," Jay said with bemusement. "Mr. Dunn has decided to move on then, has he?"

"Don't act like you didn't cause this! I want to know what you said to him!"

"I merely suggested that it might be in his best interest to move on before your *fiancé* decided to press charges for that little incident in the Diner."

"Well, that's just terrific!"

"Look," Jay said, beginning to lose his patience, "I won't sit here and be treated like this! You will calm down, Miss Maysure, or you'll find yourself sitting in my jail cell until you do!"

He could see the anger was still present in her demeanour, but she lowered her tone. "The man apologized to Larry. My fiancé had no intention of pressing charges."

"The man just purchased a stockpile of weapons and ammo," Jay said. "After speaking with Stan Hirsch and Arthur Brusard yesterday, I felt it might be best for Mr. Dunn to move on before things escalated."

Jenny was unwilling to let it go. "Did you even bother to check into Mr. Dunn before banishing him?"

"Are you really this upset over how he treated your man?" Jay scoffed.

Jenny smiled. "Not at all, *Sheriff*," she said in a tone that implied the last word was meant as an insult. "I'm simply worried that you have let a man wanted for murder go free. I wonder how that will play out in the press."

Jay was stunned into silence. Before he could find the words to respond, Jenny turned and left the station.

***

"Good riddance," Stan declared between bites of his hot beef sandwich.

Jenny had just given everyone at the table an update on the progress of her story. Larry could tell, by the expression on Mary Maysure's face that Jenny was going to get an earful about going to interview the man alone once they got home. The dinner with both of their parents had been Larry's idea, which he was beginning to regret.

Jenny twirled some spaghetti around her fork and then raised it. "How can you say that, Mr. Hirsch?" she asked before depositing the spaghetti into her mouth.

"You said it yourself," Stan replied. "The man is a potential murderer. Do you really want a person like that to stick around town?"

Mary shivered. "I certainly don't like the sound of that."

"You're both missing the point," Jenny complained. "If he is a killer, we don't know where he is anymore."

Larry stopped midway through taking a bite of his burger. "You think he's hiding somewhere around town?"

Jenny nodded. "He was so determined to find this 'Heis' guy. I know what that's like, and I'm telling you that he wouldn't give up his search if he thought he was close to finding the truth."

"Even so," Stan said, "there really isn't anything else that you can do about it."

Mary nodded in agreement. "You really should let Sheriff Chow handle this, honey."

"What if he tries to come after Larry or you, Mr. Hirsch?" Jenny's concern seemed genuine.

Larry felt like needed to support her. "Perhaps it would be a good idea to speak to the Brusard Boys about this. Maybe organize a hunt to be sure he's really gone."

Larry could see his father was furious that he had spoken, but before a stern reply could occur, Dianne dropped by with a fresh round of drinks. "Who's gone now?"

"That drifter left town," Stan said dismissively.

"Well, that's a shame," Dianne replied. "He was good for business."

"How so?" Jenny asked, ignoring the look on Stan's face.

"The man was carrying around a stack of bills taller than that salt shaker," Dianne said cheerfully. "He was a good tipper too."

"You spoke to him?"

"Sure did. He seemed like a kind fellow who just had some troubles in his past."

Stan rose and excused himself, muttering something about feeling unwell and needing to head home. Larry thought about following him but decided that it might be best to give his dad a bit of space.

"Don't we all," Jenny said, too engrossed in the conversation to notice Stan's departure. "Do you happen to know if he mentioned any plans for while he was here? Perhaps where he planned to go afterwards?"

"Can't say that I do," Dianne said, then patted Jenny's arm when she saw her face drop. "Some mysteries simply can't be solved, darling."

Dianne walked off to attend to some of her other customers. After she left, the trio returned to their meals. Mary and Jenny became engrossed in a conversation about some rare herbs that Mary had found tucked away in some obscure part of the forest the previous day. Larry couldn't focus on what they were saying though. He felt bad that the subject of the drifter and the person named Heis kept coming up. He had thought about telling Jenny not to mention it at supper, but he knew there would be no containing her excitement about what she had learned or her outrage at the scoop she had lost. Larry didn't understand why this topic upset his dad so much, but he was hopeful that now that the man had left town, the subject would disappear from the minds of the townsfolk soon as well.

I wanted to surprise your mother with my early return. I called Marsha's mother and arranged to have a spare key mailed to me so that I could do just that. The moment it arrived, I packed my things and began my trip home. Along the way I stopped several times to purchase flowers, chocolates, groceries, and a small stuffed bear for your mother. I wanted everything to be perfect. I planned to cook her a surprise pasta dinner. I even used what savings I had to rent a hotel room for the rest of her family, just so that we could have our special evening alone. I wanted it to be a night that we would remember for the rest of our lives. A night to make up for all those nights we had to live apart. A night where I would show Marsha the depth of my love for her.

Sadly, my dream was shattered when I walked through the door. As I stood there, listening to the sounds of passionate lovemaking, I felt overwhelmed by emotion. I wanted to scream with rage, to cry out in agony, and to run away all at once. All I could do though was stand there silently staring toward the bedroom. When they finished, your mother emerged from the room to find me staring blankly at her. Her face was a mixture of shock and sorrow. Marsha tried to run to me. She wanted to explain what happened, but I wouldn't listen. I threw my gifts on the floor and stormed out of the building. Sometimes I wish I had been wise enough to end our relationship that night.

CHAPTER 7

October 10, 2011

Kerry trudged bitterly through the muddy landscape. He had a great deal on his mind, and it was disrupting his enjoyment of the hunt. When he had woken up the previous morning to discover it was raining again, he had thought that the most disappointing part of his day would be having to wait another day to hunt for his bear. However, when he learned that Dunn had left town later that evening, Kerry couldn't help feeling angry. He had believed that the man, despite his secrets, thought of Kerry as a friend. Yet he couldn't even bother to stop by Kerry's home to say goodbye before leaving town. Kerry felt angry at Dunn and himself for being so foolish as to think a rich man like that would be interested in him. He had been so furious that he had barely gotten any sleep before his alarm sounded at 3:00 a.m. Though the day promised similar weather to the previous one, Kerry knew he would not be able to just sit around his place. He needed to take out his frustration on the land.

Unfortunately, the land had not been kind to him so far. He had been working his way through the forest for more than two hours now, and the only animal he had seen was a rabbit, which had managed to avoid his shots and escape into the underbrush. Kerry desperately wanted to take his pain out on some other creature. He wanted to prove to himself and to that bastard drifter that he was better than the man he had saved. He wanted to exert his dominance over something and regain his self-confidence. Kerry had not felt this inadequate since his wife left him for that bank teller.

However, the world seemed to be against his desires. As the sun crept into the sky, the clouds unleashed their fury upon him. Kerry was drenched within minutes and angrily kicked a tree, injuring his foot. Limping, he finally admitted defeat and turned to make his way back to his truck when he heard the low growl. Kerry was certain it was a bear. Though the pain in his foot was barely tolerable, he pressed on through the bushes toward the sound. Soon he came upon a set of tracks that confirmed he was chasing his long-sought quarry. Kerry said a small prayer of thanks for this turn in his luck and then crept after the animal.

Lightning crashed and thunder rumbled as Kerry emerged into a small clearing. Although he could no longer hear the bear, the storm had not yet washed its tracks away. After everything Kerry had been through, he was not going to give his prize up now. He pushed on into the clearing, trying to keep low to avoid being seen if the animal was close. However, when the tracks disappeared in the middle of the clearing, he rose to his feet and screamed.

"Shit!"

Kerry threw down his rifle and fell to his knees. He couldn't believe that after all of this he was going to return home empty-handed. He pounded the ground with both fists and screamed once more. After a few deep breaths, he rose to his feet and reached down to pick up his gun. He was fortunate that the first shot came at that instant, shattering the back of his left shoulder rather than entering through his chest. Regardless, the blow knocked Kerry over. He had no way of knowing if he had been mistaken by a hunter for an animal or targeted by an assailant, but either way, Kerry was certain that he was still in danger. He had to get to his weapon.

With tremendous effort, Kerry rolled onto his stomach and began to crawl toward his firearm. The second shot rang out as he was reaching for it, obliterating the bones in his right hand and causing Kerry to scream in pain. Realizing this was no accident, Kerry tried to get to his feet and run for the cover of the trees, but he barely made it three steps before the third shot crashed through his knee. Hearing his murderer approaching and knowing he had no chance of escape, Kerry rolled over to look up at the man.

Recognition filled his eyes. "Why?" he asked.

The fourth shot into Kerry's face was the only answer he would ever receive.

***

When Lily told Jenny about the radio call that her husband had responded to that morning, Jenny grabbed her camera and ran to her car. She raced over to where Kerry had parked his truck, cursing under her breath the whole way. She was certain that this would involve Dunn somehow, and she blamed herself for it. As she was parking, Sheriff Chow and Dr. Sindell emerged from the forest carrying a stretcher. Although there was a sheet over him, Jenny knew who was beneath it. She saw Sheriff Chow mouth the word "Shit!" as she emerged from her vehicle.

"Jenny Maysure, Barrens' Media," she said, assuming her professional role.

Jay rolled his eyes. "I know who you are, Miss Maysure."

"Then you also know that I have a job to do, sir."

"As do I," he said, clearly irritated now. "Would you move so that we can load him into Doc's car?"

Jenny obliged but did not relent on her interrogation. "Is that Mr. Giles?"

"No comment," Jay replied, trying to dismiss her.

Jenny would have none of it. "Was he murdered, Sheriff?"

Jay sighed. "Look, I'll tell you what we have so far but only if you promise to keep wild allegations like those to yourself."

Jenny nodded but caught the look of concern that passed over Dr. Sindell's face as he strapped the stretcher down. She made a mental note to check in with him later.

"Alright," Jay said, "yes, unfortunately, this is the body of Kerry Giles. His truck was seen by some hunters who were familiar with him. They tracked his movements to a nearby clearing and found his body. At this time I believe this is nothing more than a hunting accident. Publishing anything else would only serve to further upset a community that will already be devastated by this tragedy as is."

Jenny thought about protesting but decided this wasn't the time. "Mind if I take some photos for the paper?" she asked.

"I'm not letting you take pictures of the body," Jay said, "but I suppose there's no harm in you going to have a look at the scene if you like. I'll be filing my report with the city authorities on this matter when I get back to town."

With that both men hopped into the doctor's large station wagon, leaving Jenny standing there with more questions than answers. Regardless of what the sheriff said, one thing was for sure, this definitely had something to do with Dunn. Jenny wasn't going to rest until she found out what his connection was.

***

As soon as Sheriff Chow called him, Ike had asked his assistant to cancel his appointments for the day. Ike knew that the sheriff would want his report on the autopsy of Kerry Giles as soon as possible. While he had a general understanding of the process, it was not something that he had trained for, so Ike expected that it would take some time to complete. Also, it was clear to him that there was some friction between Jenny and the sheriff, and it would be best for things to be concluded in this matter as soon as possible.

Unfortunately, several hours later, Ike found himself torn by what he saw. He realized now, as he had feared earlier, that things were not as cut and dried as the sheriff had hoped. Kerry had a remarkable number of injuries for this to be just a hunting accident. Ike couldn't help wondering how a person could not have heard Kerry cry out after the first shot hit him. Ike likewise could not understand how the wound to Kerry's hand could have been made so precisely, particularly since the bullet entered the backside of it. Ike believed that such a wound could only have occurred up close, which was confirmed by the final shot to his face, and that meant that Kerry was intentionally killed. However, if Ike concluded this, it would surely cause the panic that Sheriff Chow had alluded to earlier in the day. Ike was so torn by his internal conflict that he did not notice Jenny slip into the room behind him.

"Something weighing on your mind, Doctor?" she asked sweetly, causing him to nearly jump out of his skin.

"Miss Maysure," Ike stammered. "I didn't hear you come in."

"You also didn't answer my question," Jenny stated.

"Right," Ike said. "I don't have anything troubling me, so you need not worry."

"That's interesting," Jenny said, stepping closer to him and the body, "because when we were in the woods earlier today, I could have sworn you looked concerned when the sheriff suggested that Kerry was killed in a hunting accident."

"Concerned?" Ike said, beginning to sweat. "Not at all."

"I guess it must have been my imagination," Jenny said.

Ike sighed, relieved to have fooled her, or so he thought. Looking up, he realized she was now standing over the body. He could see that she was studying it, and he knew there would be no hiding the truth now.

"You know what I found odd about the scene of the 'accident', Doctor?" Jenny continued.

"I can't say," he replied, his voice trembling.

"I found it odd that Kerry made it so far."

"Pardon me?" Ike asked, genuinely confused.

"Well, it seems to me that Kerry was first shot closer to the middle of the clearing. That's not where you found his body though, is it?"

"No," Ike gasped.

"I didn't think so," Jenny replied, smirking. "Tell me, Doctor, how many times was Kerry Giles shot before he died?"

"Four." Ike felt tears begin to stream down his face.

"Four," Jenny scoffed. "That's some accident."

She began to walk out of the room. "What are you going to do?" Ike called after her.

"You'll have to read about it in tomorrow's paper, Doctor, just like everybody else."

Upon returning to my father's house, I found him waiting up with a large glass of whiskey. He poured me one, drained his own, then refilled his glass. Then he began to tell me how disloyal Marsha had been. My father told me that he had hired a private investigator to keep tabs on her shortly after my first term in college began. He wanted to prove that everything he had said about her was true, but he could not have imagined how low she'd sink. He had learned that she had been having an affair with Jake Finester, the punter from my high school football team. The boy had no real talent besides his kick, which he lost as a result of an injury during our final season. Jake could barely hold down a job now and wasted most of his days drinking with Marsha's brother.

My father said this had been going on for a long time, but he had not mentioned it before because he feared it would affect my studies. Now that I had discovered the affair for myself, however, my father insisted that it was a matter of family pride that we resolve this. Then he offered me a choice. I could forgive and marry the woman who had dishonoured the Heis name, or she could join Jake in the fate that befalls anybody who trifled with one of the founding families. Despite what she had done, I still loved Marsha, and did not think I could live without her. I made my choice.

CHAPTER 8

October 11, 2011

Jenny was beaming with pride when she walked into Barrens' Media the following morning. Cody had been less than impressed when she had called him in after hours and demanded the morning edition be reprinted. However, once he read what she had, Cody could not deny the importance of letting the community know that there could be a murderer in their midst. He was a bit more skeptical about her desire to name Dunn as a suspect but allowed her to include a profile about him as long as she didn't outright accuse him of anything.

As she walked by Lily, however, the snicker she heard instantly soured her mood.

"Do you have something to say?" Jenny snapped.

"Not at all," Lily replied smugly. "But my husband will be here soon to share a few words."

As soon as Jenny stepped into her office and closed the door, the main doors to the building were flung open with a crash.

"Barrens!" Jay shouted.

Cody took his time emerging from his office. "Is something wrong, Sheriff?"

Jay walked over to Jenny's office and slammed the paper down on her desk. "How dare you print this?"

Cody shook his head. "Is anything we reported untrue?"

Shaking with rage, Jay pointed at Jenny. "I told you not to spread wild allegations about a murderer in our town!"

Cody refused to be ignored. "Was Kerry Giles shot to death or not, Sheriff?"

"Yes, he was shot and, yes, it was four fucking times. But that does not mean it is in any way connected to this Dunn character! I looked into your 'reporter's' claims about him having a warrant, and guess what I found? Absolutely nothing!"

Cody shot a furious glance toward Jenny. "I swear my cousin at the FBI—"

"We'll discuss this later," Cody growled and then returned his attention to the sheriff. "I'll have a retraction printed."

"See to it that you do!" Jay shouted as he left.

**

Larry could hear Jenny's screams of outrage before he entered the house. As he had anticipated, her article must have touched a nerve with the sheriff. Larry took a deep breath and then walked through the outer door.

"Hello honey," he called cheerfully.

Larry was surprised to see Mrs. Maysure instead of his fiancée greet him in the mudroom. "You'd better prepare for a rough night, son," she said as she headed past him out the door.

"Did you lie to me, Derek?" Jenny yelled into the phone as Larry entered the kitchen.

Knowing it was best not to interrupt her, Larry leaned in and kissed her on the cheek. Then he took a seat at the table to wait for things to unfold.

"You told me that you found a warrant for Dunn!" Jenny's face turned bright red. "What do you mean the case is closed? How the fuck could he be arrested over two thousand miles away from here yesterday when he was here two days before that? Fuck you!'"

Jenny slammed the phone down and kicked a chair over. Larry leaped up and embraced her before she could do any more damage.

"Let me go, Larry," Jenny warned.

"Not until you agree to stop taking out your anger on your mom's kitchen," Larry replied with a chuckle.

He realized he had grossly misread the situation when Jenny shoved him away. "Do you think this is funny, Larry?"

"Sweetie, I'm sorry..."

"My career could be at stake, and you're cracking jokes?"

He tried to go to her again, but she slapped him.

"My credibility is completely shot now!" Jenny raged. "I wish that son of a bitch never came to town!"

Larry was stunned. Jenny had never hit him in the six years that they had been together. Part of him knew that this wasn't about him, and another part knew that she still needed him right now, but those fell short of his own outrage.

"How dare you!" Larry yelled.

Jenny shrank back at his words, but she was not intimidated for long. "Fuck you, Larry!"

Larry turned and walked over to the mudroom to put his boots back on. He half hoped that she would follow him and apologize for what she had done, but he wasn't surprised when she didn't. Grabbing his coat, he stepped out into the chilly autumn night.

***

Dianne hummed a tune as she tidied up the lunch counter at the Diner. It had been another day of good business and great meals. Nothing pleased Dianne more than hearing her patrons' compliments about her food and service. She also loved the stories her customers told her in return. The vacationing hunters brought tales of faraway lands while the locals kept her in touch with everything that took place in Traders' Point. The days were long and the nights even longer, but she took pride in the service that she provided her town.

"Don't forget to lock the door, Ma," Kennedy said as he stepped into the bathroom with the mop and bucket.

Dianne smiled but remained in place and continued to hum her tune. She enjoyed how her boy fussed over his mam now as she had done when he and his sister were children. Gathering the last tray of dirty dishes, she made her way into the kitchen. She placed the dishes next to the large sink and began to run the water. Then she returned the last of the vegetables lying out on the cutting board to the cold storage before returning to the sink to add some soap. She was midway through cleanup when Kennedy walked in with a heavy black bag of garbage slung over his shoulder.

"Everything is tidied up out front," he said with a tired smile.

Dianne leaned over and kissed him on the cheek. "You're a good lad. Toss that in the trash and then head home, baby."

Kennedy looked like he wanted to protest but did not have the energy to do so. He simply nodded, and Dianne smiled. A sudden crash outside caused Dianne to drop the glass she had been washing. Kennedy dropped the garbage and ran outside, cursing about the animals as he did so. Dianne listened to him swear and chuckled to herself before kneeling down to pick up the shards of broken glass scattered around her feet. The sound of the bell at the front door made her freeze in place.

"I'm sorry, honey," she called out, feeling unnerved, "but we closed a half an hour ago!"

Dianne listened carefully for the sound of the bell once more. There was silence for a few minutes, and her fears grew in the stillness as the seconds ticked by. Perhaps Kennedy had been right about locking up. Thoughts of what had happened to Kerry the previous day ran through her mind. Dianne was about to go out back to ask Kennedy to deal with the customer when the bell sounded once more. Laughing at her silliness but still feeling nervous, Dianne abandoned her task and quickly walked out front to lock the door.

In her haste, Dianne did not notice the figure crouching behind the lunch counter with a hunting knife. She peered out the door but didn't see anybody in the dark. Sighing with relief, she turned the key in the lock and felt safe. The moment of peace did not last though. A rough hand clasped her around her mouth. It was followed by a rush of pain throughout her body as the knife was plunged into her back. Dianne struggled in her assailant's grip as he stabbed her several more times before she managed to land a lucky elbow into his ribs. Feeling his grip loosen, she kicked him in the shin and broke free.

"Bitch!" he exclaimed as he fell against the counter, knocking over several chairs.

"Help!" Dianne screamed as she tried to flee, but the pain in her back forced her to her knees after a single step.

She began to crawl toward the kitchen, but she did not reach the door. A hand grabbed her by her hair and yanked her back into the blade once more. As it pierced her throat, she spat blood all over the shiny tile floor. Then he lifted her up and slammed her onto a table in one of the booths. It broke beneath her, and she crumpled to the floor.

Dianne began to fade in and out then. She heard the chime of the clock as it struck midnight. Then she saw the image of her killer approaching with the blade raised to finish the job. A loud noise in the back seemed to startle her attacker. Then he was gone, and Kennedy was standing over her.

"Mom!" she heard him cry as the world began to spin. "I'll run and get the doctor!"

She tried to reach for him, wanting to tell him to stay, but he was already gone. Then the darkness swallowed her final conscious thoughts of love and concern for her boy.

Within three weeks my father's words had become a reality. His first step in restoring our family's honour was to see that Jake Finester disappeared from town. I did not have the stomach to ask my father if he had paid the boy to leave or had him eliminated entirely. I was simply grateful for the opportunity to reconnect with your mother. In the beginning she was reluctant to rekindle our relationship, but after a few weeks together things began to feel as they once had. I began to have hope that, given time, our love would become as strong as it had been before I left for college.

Alas, things were not moving at a pace which pleased my father. Around this time he announced our engagement in the papers and declared that we were to be wed by the end of the month. Marsha was far from happy with this arrangement, and she made certain to let me know it. I tried to negotiate with my father, but he would have none of it. Marsha continued to complain about his interference in our affairs, but after a word with my father in his office one night, she grew silent on the matter. Our wedding ceremony was tense, and I feared that she might leave me. I mentioned these concerns to my father, who had a house built for us outside of the city as a wedding present. This seemed to ease the tension somewhat. I knew Marsha was displeased with me, but I held out hope that, in time, she would be able to forgive me and remember the love she had for me once.

CHAPTER 8

October 12, 2011

Shitstorm! Jay thought.

It was the only word that he could use to describe the situation he currently found himself in. A large crowd had gathered outside of the Diner, largely alerted to the incident by Kennedy Smythe's cries of anguish when Dr. Sindell had informed him that his mother was dead. Jay had managed to talk the Brusard boys into standing guard, saying that they would be helping to preserve the memory of Dianne Smythe, but there was only so much that two young men and their aging uncle could do to keep the close to one hundred people from pushing their way inside. Of course, Lily and Jenny were competing to be the first to get a word from him about what was going on inside as well, and Jay knew that if he didn't give them something soon, he would lose control of the situation entirely.

The trouble was, Jay had no idea what to tell the citizens of Traders' Point. The Diner looked like something out of a horror movie. Dianne had clearly been surprised by her attacker while she was locking up, as the keys were still hanging loosely from the lock. The path of overturned furniture and blood splatter showed Jay that she had put up one hell of a fight, but Dianne had been outmatched by somebody stronger and, in all likelihood, much larger than she was. Despite all his years in law enforcement, during which he'd seen many bodies ravaged by animals and the weather, the sight of Dianne's corpse made Jay want to throw up. He swallowed hard as he approached Dr. Sindell, who had been the one to call him in.

"This is getting out of hand, Jay," Ike said without looking up from his task. "I'm not qualified to do the kind of forensics that you need for something like this."

"I'm afraid we're shit out of luck with that anyway," Jay said solemnly. "Your efforts to save Dianne, combined with her son's tracks throughout the place, have ruined any chance of lifting accurate prints. On top of that, I assume the Diner was left unattended when the kid ran over to your place, so anybody could have walked in and contaminated any evidence we could have found. No, Doctor, I am afraid this crime scene is completely fucked."

Ike ran a hand through his thinning hair and stood up. "This entire situation is fucked. Two dead bodies in as many days."

"Don't do that!" Jay snapped.

Ike recoiled as if he had been struck. "I'm sorry," he muttered.

"We have two completely different crime scenes and two different methods of murder," Jay said, matter-of-factly. "So, unless you've found something to link the two together..."

Ike hung his head. "No. Nothing."

"Then let's not go starting any more rumours that will make their way into the town's paper, alright?"

"Yes," Ike reluctantly agreed. "So, what will you do then?"

"Unfortunately," Jay said with a sigh, feeling the weight of his position, "there's only one thing I can do right now to defuse the situation."

With that he stepped out the front door.

***

Word of Dianne's death spread like wildfire throughout Traders' Point. Some people had just been settling in for the night while others had been in bed for hours, but they had all turned out to see what had befallen an icon of their community. With some effort Jenny had wormed her way through the crowd to stand beside Lily, who held a microphone attached to a small recorder in her other hand, awaiting the formal announcement from her husband of what had taken place. Jenny saw Kennedy sitting on a stump with his head in his hands, sobbing with grief. A hunter from out of town was standing next to him, armed with a shotgun, undoubtedly at Sheriff Chow's request. This reignited her anger at everything that had happened the previous day.

"Your husband cannot seriously think that Kennedy killed his mother~" Jenny shouted at Lily over the noise of the crowd.

Lily simply grinned and mouthed the words "No comment." Jenny clenched her fists but kept her anger hidden from her face. Taking out her notepad, she took a look around the crowd and then wrote down a few observations. The Brusard family had clearly been deputized to handle crowd control, and Jenny suspected that Dr. Sindell would be inside with the body. She would be sure to speak to him later. Then she began to make notes about the crowd's reaction. She paused when she spied Larry and his father standing off to the side of the group. Jenny thought about going over to apologize to her man but gave that up as soon as the door to the Diner swung open. Lily seized upon Jenny's hesitation and stepped up as quickly as a jackrabbit with her microphone.

"What's going on in there, Sheriff?" she asked in a voice that was somehow sweet and professional at the same time.

"It appears that Ms. Smythe was attacked inside during the late hours of the previous evening," Jay said grimly. "Sadly, she did not survive this attack."

Kennedy cried out in grief when Jay spoke those words. His agonizing screams broke Jenny's heart, and she instantly regretted how cruel she had been toward her mother and Larry earlier. Had one of them been the victim instead, she would not have been able to cope with her actions. The people of Traders' Point seemed equally devastated by this, with the exception of Lily, who pressed on with the standard line of questions.

"Can you expand any further on what took place, Sheriff?"

"At this time all I'm willing to say is that this killing was very personal in nature."

"Was a gun used in the attack, Sheriff?" Jenny piped up, hoping to make a link to her previous story without revealing her motives.

"Actually, Miss Maysure, Dianne Smythe was stabbed to death," Jay replied through gritted teeth.

Lily failed to note his change in expression. "Did the killer take the weapon with him, Sheriff?"

"No," Jay replied, exasperated. "The knife was left behind."

"Were you able to get any fingerprints?" Jenny chimed in.

"Unfortunately, the scene was contaminated by the attempts to save Ms. Smythe's life. It's unlikely that we will be able to get any usable evidence."

"What would you suggest the citizens of Traders' Point do at this time, Sheriff?" Lily asked.

Jay took a deep breath. "At this time the best thing any of us can do is return to our homes and make sure our children are tucked in safely. If anybody happened to witness anything that took place, I would ask that they come to speak to me in the morning."

His tone seemed to suggest a finality to the interview, and the crowd began to turn to disperse. Jenny wasn't satisfied yet though. Deep down she felt certain that these deaths were connected, and she wasn't about to let an opportunity to challenge the sheriff on this slip.

"Are you suggesting that a killer might be stalking our community Sheriff?"

"I'm not suggesting anything of the sort, Miss Maysure," he replied bitterly.

"Does that mean you have some proof to indicate that you're absolutely certain the death of Ms. Smythe is not connected to the tragedy that befell Kerry Giles recently?"

Jenny thought she'd struck gold. Everyone had been drawn back in by their discussion. All eyes were on the sheriff now, and Jenny was certain that he would have no choice but to admit that he'd been wrong earlier about his denial of her story. Jay shifted uncomfortably under their gaze but said nothing for several moments. Jenny savoured every second of his plight, satisfied that karma was about to repay him for his attack on her. Then Jenny's face fell as she saw him pull a pair of handcuffs off of his belt.

He walked over to where Kennedy was sitting. "I'm hereby placing you under arrest for the murder of Dianne Smythe," he declared reluctantly.

The crowd around Jenny erupted with emotions ranging from disbelief to rage. The Brusard family stood firm in their roles as deputies despite the efforts of the people to press forward toward the accused. Jenny, however, stood in place, worried that she and Kennedy might spend the rest of their lives regretting the last question she'd asked.

***

Ike sat in the corner of the small, damp basement chain smoking for the first time in nearly twenty years. Periodically, he would burst into fits of coughing that reminded him why he had quit in the first place. Now was not the time to address those concerns though. Ike knew that he would need the support of the nicotine to help him cope with the task at hand. Unfortunately, it was becoming increasingly clear to Ike that the cigarettes were not having their desired effect, as the body of Dianne Smythe lay untouched on the slab across the room.

Ike had decided that it would be best to convert the basement of his modest home into a makeshift morgue after Kerry was killed. He wanted not only to preserve the body but also to keep it in a place where it would not affect the patients attending his practice. However, as the chill of the room clung to his skin in the dim lighting, he began to regret his decision. The eerie setting reminded him of the many horror films his friends in university had insisted he watch with them. He always hated how cliché the morgues in those movies looked right up until the point when the doctor was killed by the psychopath or monster. Ike shivered at the thought.

He rose, freshly lit cigarette in hand, and began to pace back and forth in front of the body. Ike knew what he needed to do and that he was the only person in town with the skills to do so, but he still couldn't work up the nerve to get on with it. After all, this was Dianne Smythe.

Kerry's autopsy had been tough, but it was not nearly so emotional for him as this would be. After all, the man had only been a patient of his, and Ike never really felt very close to him. They'd never shared a meal at each other's homes or spent any time together outside of his office. In fact, Ike was not very close to any of the hunters living in the area and, had his sister not mentioned the opening for a new physician in town, Ike likely would have ended up in some city far away from there.

However, Dianne was different. She had been a pillar of the community. Everyone felt close to her, and everyone had visited the Diner regularly, not just for the convenient food but also for the charm that Dianne brought to every person who walked through her door. Nobody could remain angry or sad once they saw her smile. She had been the friendliest and kindest person that Ike had ever met and, though the body that lay before him no longer held her spirit, a sense of finality still came with doing her autopsy that Ike was struggling to come to terms with.

A loud coughing from the top of the stairs alerted Ike to his niece's presence. "Is there a fire down there, Dr. Sindell?" Brittany asked, her voice full of concern.

Ike quickly put out his cigarette and rushed over to meet her at the bottom of the stairs. "Nothing to worry about, dear."

"Okay," she replied with a knowing grin. "Just make sure my mom doesn't catch you doing that, or she'll kill us both."

Ike chuckled. "I promise. Did you need something?"

Brittany's smile faded. "Sheriff Chow keeps calling for updates about Dianne's autopsy. He seems really insistent on filing the paperwork today for Kennedy Smythe's transfer."

The low rumble of an approaching storm made Ike smile slyly. "Sounds like there won't be much of a hurry."

His joke did little to cheer his niece. "Do you really think that Ken killed his mom?"

Seeing the pain in Brittany's eyes, Ike felt terrible. She had grown up with Kennedy, and they had spent many hours together during their youth. Ike realized that, as hard as this whole thing was for him, it must be infinitely worse for the young lady standing in front of him. He wanted to comfort her but was wary of giving her false hope.

"No," he admitted reluctantly.

"Then why is Sheriff Chow putting him in jail?" Brittany cried, bursting into tears.

Ike pulled her into his arms. "I don't know, Brittany. Perhaps he just wanted to make sure that things didn't get out of hand last night."

"It's not fair!" she wept. "I love him!"

This revelation surprised Ike. He had not even been aware that the two had begun to see each other romantically. "I'm sorry darling but there—"

"You have to help him, Uncle Ike," she pleaded. "I'm going to have his child."

Ike pulled away from her in shock. "Does your mother know about this?"

Brittany shook her head. "I haven't even had a chance to tell Kennedy yet."

"I'll do what I can," I said, torn between his professional duties and his love for his niece.

Brittany smiled slightly through her tears. "Thank you," she whispered.

"Go upstairs and tell the sheriff that I'll speak with him at his office in the morning," Ike replied, resuming his professional tone and straightening his tie. "Now let me be, please. I have a lot of work to do."

Our honeymoon could not have been more fantastic. We flew to Europe in the middle of the night about a month after our wedding. Marsha's depression seemed to lift the moment our plane left the ground. We spent the next three months travelling through France, Germany, Switzerland, Spain, and England. I spent thousands of dollars on fancy hotels, elegant clothes, and dinners at the finest restaurants. Though I cared little for these things, they seemed to please your mother, and I cared deeply for her well-being. During those months together, our relationship became stronger than it had ever been, and I cannot recall a happier time in my life.

Sadly, my father was growing weary of my lack of commitment to the Heis legacy and insisted on making sure that I learned my place upon our return. To correct my lack of focus, he promoted me to a position with greater responsibility in the company. This meant longer hours at the factory and frequently resulted in me taking work home. Gradually, I began to pull all-nighters and could go days without spending more than a few minutes at a time with Marsha.

It wasn't long before these changes began to impact your mother's mood. Once more she began to complain about how much control my father had over our lives. She demanded that we leave the city to make a life of our own. As much as I desired to do this, I knew my father would never allow it. When things did not change, Marsha began to talk about moving out and divorcing me. I shared these concerns with my father, and he told me that he would set things straight. After several visits to my home while I was working, Marsha's complaints faded into silence. From that point forward, she looked at me with nothing but disdain.

CHAPTER 9

October 13, 2011

The last twenty-four hours had been hell for Jay. Although he knew that Jenny and his wife were only doing their jobs, they had forced his hand, and it had blown up in his face. If he had actually wanted to investigate the Diner for clues, he would not have been able to do so because a steady stream of townsfolk and visiting hunters alike had dropped by the station to complain about his decision to charge Kennedy with the crime.

In truth, Jay had to admit that he didn't believe the boy had the stomach for it. However, there was nobody else that he could place at the scene of the crime. Even worse, Jay knew that, were he to admit his doubts publicly, it would also mean having to admit the likelihood that a killer was stalking their town. While he expected that some people would assume that Jenny was right about this rogue giant stalking their town, Jay believed it was equally likely that they would begin to suspect each other as well. He could not see how causing that sort of panic would benefit anyone other than the killer.

Jay sipped a mug of coffee as he listened to the rain hammer against his office window. He prayed silently to his ancestors that today would be easier. The boom of the main doors to the precinct told him that wouldn't be the case.

"Chow!" a familiar voice exclaimed as thunder boomed outside.

Jay sighed and walked into the main area of the police station to find Dr. Sindell, drenched and his face flushed with anger, standing before him. "Coffee?" Jay asked calmly.

"Coffee?" Ike screamed. "How can you think of coffee at a time like this?"

Jay shrugged and took a long sip from his own mug before speaking again. "I take it you finished the autopsy on Dianne?"

Dr. Sindell shook the folder in his hand. "She was murdered with a knife!"

"I figured that," Jay said, beginning to lose his patience. "I was hoping you could tell me something that wasn't obvious."

Ike clenched his teeth. "Dianne was attacked from behind. I suspect that the wound to her throat was the last one to be delivered. However, before the killer could finish the job, I suspect that he fled the Diner since she died as a result of blood loss."

"I suppose you think the killer stopped because Kennedy interrupted him?" Jay asked.

"Of course he did!" Ike exploded. "What other possibility is there?"

"Perhaps he realized he would be accused and decided to try to make it look like he wanted to save her."

"Are you fucking mad, Chow?"

"Sheriff Chow!"

"Whatever!" Ike had completely lost control now. "What possible reason could you have for suspecting the boy?"

Jay ticked the points off on his fingers as he replied. "He was the first person on the scene, he sought you out before me and ensured that all of the evidence would be lost in your attempts to save her, he stands to inherit the Diner now that she is gone, and he was covered in her blood."

"So was I!" Ike shouted.

"Then maybe I should arrest you as well!" Jay replied, matching the doctor's anger.

Jay saw the fight instantly leave Ike's eyes. He sighed and put the folder down on a nearby table. "She put up a fight, Sheriff."

"What?"

"Dianne fought against her killer. If the boy did this, he would surely have some injuries, but I don't recall observing any, do you?"

Ike went out, leaving Jay standing there with nothing except for a renewed confidence in his own doubts.

***

As the storm raged around her vehicle, Jenny regretted her decision to wait until today to confront the sheriff. She had known that the people of Traders' Point would rally to defend Kennedy, and she thought it would be better to wait until after some of that pressure died down. Instead, Jenny had focused on quietly inquiring around town about the various places that the drifter had visited during his stay in town. She had managed to confirm the sheriff's story about the weapons that Dunn had purchased from the Brusard boys. Even though her cousin's lead had fallen through, Jenny still believed that Maverick Dunn was somehow responsible for Kerry and Dianne's deaths. The weapons and his disappearance made him the number one suspect in her book. Although she wanted to play a part in catching him, what Jenny feared more was whom the Dunn might target next.

Jenny parked her vehicle and ran toward the doors of the police station. She stopped short of entering though when she heard raised voices over the howling wind. She recognized Sheriff Chow's voice immediately, but it took her a few minutes to figure out who the other belonged to. Jenny was surprised when she realized that it was Dr. Sindell who was yelling at the sheriff. The doctor was a rather timid man, and she could not recall a time she'd ever heard him raise his voice. Jenny propped the door open slightly to listen to what was being said. When she realized that Dr. Sindell was there to go after the sheriff for locking up Kennedy, as she had intended to, Jenny stepped away to wait until they were finished.

She had planned to intimidate the sheriff into letting her speak with the boy, but she had serious doubts that would work now. Instead, as soon as she saw Dr. Sindell leave, Jenny slipped into the building and turned on the charm.

"Rough morning, Sheriff?" she asked sweetly.

"I'm not in the mood to argue with you, Miss Maysure," he grumbled.

"Nor am I," Jenny replied. "I just thought you might like a bit of help is all."

Jay laughed. "What possible help could I need from a journalist?"

Jenny buried her contempt for his insult of her profession and continued. "It seems to me that there are a lot of people questioning your handling of this case."

"So, what's that got to do with you?"

"Well, I was just thinking that this situation with the Smythe murder seems like a tough spot, and perhaps getting something on the record might sway the people of Traders' Point to give you a break."

Jay wasn't fooled. "If you think I'm going to let you in there to talk to that boy, you're out of your mind."

"Now let's not be hasty, Sheriff," Jenny said. "After all, I highly doubt the boy is going to open up to you now that you've arrested him."

"I don't need his confession," Jay said, glaring at her.

"You have some evidence to tie him to this then?" Jenny asked.

A flash of concern passed over Jay's face, but then he recovered. "That's none of your concern."

"True," Jenny said, "but I'll gladly be there to cover the story when Kennedy sues you for false imprisonment."

"Bitch!"

"There's no call for that, Sheriff," Jenny replied sweetly. "Now, are you going to let me in to speak with him?"

***

As Jenny stepped into the small space that served as an interrogation room, she could not help noticing how little it resembled what she'd seen on TV. The walls were painted a cheerful yellow and were covered in framed photos of landscapes found in the area. Additionally, the room had a wide window. As a result of the storm, a candle had been lit in the centre of the cheap wooden table. Kennedy sat on the opposite side of the table, his head hung low, sobbing quietly. His ankles were attached to the legs of the table by chains, and his wrists were bound in front of him with handcuffs. Even though he had only been there for a day, the boy looked like he hadn't seen a shower or meal in a week.

"Ten minutes," Jay said bitterly as he closed the door behind her.

"Good morning, Kennedy," Jenny said as she sat down.

"I'm afraid there are no more good mornings," Kennedy replied glumly.

Jenny reached across the table and held his hands in hers. "I am truly sorry about what happened to your mother, Kennedy."

"Ken," he whispered. "Please call me 'Ken.' My mother was the only one who insisted on calling me 'Kennedy.'"

This admission brought forth fresh tears from the boy, and Jenny swallowed hard. "Okay, Ken. Do you think you could talk to me about what happened?"

He looked up at her for the first time, his features reflecting how much he'd aged recently. "Are you looking to blame this on me too?"

"I'm looking for the truth, Ken," Jenny replied. "And if you're innocent, I'll do everything I can to get you out of here. Does that sound fair to you?"

He eyed her skeptically at first but then sighed in defeat. "That's more than anyone else is offering me. I really don't know what to tell you though."

"Why don't you start at the beginning?" Jenny suggested.

"It was a typical night," he said. "We were cleaning up and getting ready to go home."

"Okay. Where was your mom?"

"She was in the kitchen doing the dishes. I had just finished cleaning the bathrooms and was about to take the trash outside."

"Did you go outside?"

"Not at first." Kennedy stifled a sob. "Mom and I talked for a bit. She was worried about how tired I was, and she wanted me to go home."

"Then what happened?"

"A fucking raccoon knocked over the trash." Kennedy began crying again. "I went outside to clean up the mess and left her all alone!"

"So, we're talking about you being outside for, what, ten minutes?"

Kennedy shook his head. "That's the weird thing. All of the cans were overturned. It was as if they had been knocked over like dominoes. It took me close to twenty minutes to clean everything up."

Jenny made sure to note this. Knowing that animals could be a problem in Traders' Point, everyone had invested in cans with locking mechanisms. There was no way that an animal could have spilled all of them. She didn't want the boy to know that she suspected the killer had done this to distract him. He was blaming himself enough already for what happened.

"Go on," she said.

"When I went back inside, I . . . found . . . her." Kennedy broke down.

Jenny wanted to comfort him, but she knew her time was running out, and there was one more thing she needed to know. "This is really important, Ken. I need you to focus.

He looked up at her through tears and nodded.

"Did you see anybody slip by you while you were cleaning up out back?"

"No," he whispered. "I think she must have forgotten to lock the front door again."

"Time's up!" Jay said, opening the door.

***

It had been a rough night, as he expected they all would be now that Dianne was dead. Hank's wife had been very close to the woman. They shared cooking tips, visited each other whenever they could, and even took vacations together. Sue Lawson had fallen apart when Sheriff Chow arrested Kennedy for killing his mother. Although Hank could believe it, he knew better than to say that to his wife. She had been crying constantly since then, and the only thing that seemed to bring her any reprieve were the tranquilizers that Dr. Sindell had prescribed her.

Hank had spent the last two days trying to tend to his wife's needs as well as those of their guests. It had been exhausting. Hank wasn't sure how much longer he could keep it up. As he nursed a large glass of whiskey, he considered whether or not it would be worth the cost to hire somebody to clean the lodges each day. He was starting to doze in his armchair when an odd noise drew his attention to the back door. With hazy eyes, Hank thought he saw the knob begin to turn. He rose on less than steady legs and walked toward it.

Both men were equally surprised when the door opened. Hank wasn't sure if he was dreaming or hallucinating until he saw the gun. His survival instincts kicked in then, and Hank dove toward his armchair as the intruder fired two shots from a revolver at him. He was lucky, as only the first bullet had struck him in his left thigh. Even luckier for Hank was that he happened to be a man who always kept his gun close by. The intruder entered the living room to finish the job and then froze in place, clearly surprised when he saw the shotgun, but the alcohol had slowed Hank's movements enough that he missed the first shot.

When Hank got to his knees and peered around the corner, he just barely avoided being shot in the head. He dropped to the floor and fired another shot in response as he caught a glimpse of the intruder running for the door. He heard a grunt in response and thought he had struck the man, but when he got back to his knees, Hank could no longer see his attacker. He wasn't foolish enough to assume this was over though. Grabbing a couple of extra shells, Hank reloaded his weapon and crept toward the kitchen.

The open door felt foreboding to him. He thought about shutting it and phoning the sheriff. Hank could not let this man embarrass him in front of the townsfolk though. With a fresh dose of courage, he entered the kitchen and checked behind the counters. Finding nothing, he breathed a sigh of relief and staggered over to the door.

In his current state, Hank had failed to see the broom that his attacker had overturned. He tumbled through the open doorway and down the back stairs. His weapon flew out of his hands and landed several feet away. Hank cursed under his breath, but before he could, cold metal struck the back of his head.

***

When he came to, Hank found himself tied down to his armchair. His nose was overwhelmed by the scent of gasoline, and he felt true fear then. Looking around wildly, he spotted the intruder standing in the corner smoking a cigarette. Although he couldn't tell who the man was in the darkness, Hank thought his attacker seemed familiar. Knowing he was about to die anyway, he decided to ask one final question.

"Why?" he gasped as the man lit a match.

"Because you know," he replied before tossing it onto Hank and walking out the back door.

As the flames began to consume him and everything he loved, even Hank's screams of agony were not enough to wake his wife.

I was ecstatic when your mother told me that she was pregnant with you a few weeks later. I had always wanted to be a father and longed to hold you in my arms. However, my excitement turned to horror when your mother insisted that I take her for an abortion. I could not understand why Marsha would not want to bring you into the world, and I was mortified when she said that she hated me so much that the thought of having our child made her physically sick.

Regardless of my feelings on the matter, I knew an abortion would not be possible. My father would not be able to forgive such an act. After all, the most important thing in the world to him was our family's legacy. He would surely see this act as an assault on that legacy. I was certain that he would cut us off financially or worse if I let Marsha go through with her desires. Your mother begged me not to tell him, but I wanted you more than anything I had ever wanted before. I called my father to share the wonderful news, knowing there would be no turning back once I did.

In response to my choice, Marsha sealed herself in our bedroom and denied me access until I agreed to allow her brother to move in with us. Even after I agreed, she refused to speak to me. In fact, her brother would only let me enter the room to bring her food and attend the appointments with the doctor whom my father hired to provide her care. Once Marsha managed to convince Maverick to locate a midwife for her, I was denied these little pleasures as well.

CHAPTER 10

October 14, 2011

Before making his way to the centre of town to address the people of Traders' Point, Jay needed a moment alone to collect his thoughts. He decided to walk by the smouldering ruins of Hank and Sue Lawson's home, not because he wanted to be there but because he knew nobody else would want to be.

The alarm was raised at around 1:00 a.m., though Jay believed the ranch house had likely been burning for well over an hour by that point. By the time an effort could be organized to put out the flames, the entire lower floor had been engulfed, and the building was already on the verge of collapsing. Despite this, the citizens of Traders' Point had truly come together to try to put out the blaze. Stan Hirsch had even run into the building and managed to pull Sue out of the room upstairs. She was alive, but she had suffered fairly severe burns and was unconscious. Dr. Sindell had moved her to his office and, as of now, she was still hanging on.

Unfortunately, this was where the positive news ended. The buckets of dirt and garden hoses hooked up to the outdoor faucets of the cabins were never going to be enough to put out the fire. If Jay was honest with himself, he felt that they were lucky to contain the flames to a single building. A heavy rain had begun to fall about forty-five minutes after the townsfolk began their efforts, and that had been their saving grace.

Sadly, the tragic news did not end there. Once they were able to enter the ruins of the structure, they learned that Hank had been far less fortunate than his wife. It appeared that he had fallen asleep in his recliner in the heart of the fire. Upon discovering him, Jay suspected Hank had passed out while smoking and that had likely been the cause of the blaze. After all, Hank was known for keeping an ample supply of alcohol and gasoline on his property, and these had undoubtedly contributed to his demise. Jay could only hope that the man had slept through the worst of it and passed away with minimal pain. With Dr. Sindell concentrating on trying to keep Sue alive, combined with the fact that they wouldn't be able to get any emergency vehicles into the area until the storm passed, Jay knew it would be some time before his suspicions about Hank's death could be confirmed.

A familiar hand clasped him gently on the shoulder. "It's time to go, baby," Lily said, tears in her eyes.

Jay nodded and then followed her back toward town.

***

Jay swallowed hard as he looked at the worried and angry faces of the citizens of Traders' Point. He knew he had to say something to address their fears. He also knew that nothing he could say would ever be enough.

"We have been through a lot this week," he began.

"Are we in danger?" a panicked voice asked.

"Is Sue Lawson going to be alright?" asked another.

"Everybody please calm down," Jay said. "At this point I see no reason for anyone to panic."

"Tell Hank Lawson that!" Jay thought the comment was from one of the Brusard boys, but he could not be certain of it. He decided to ignore it.

"This was nothing more than a tragic accident. The fire seems to have started around Hank. I suspect that he accidentally fell asleep while smoking."

There was a low murmur of disapproval, but Jay couldn't distinguish any particular comments amongst the crowd, so he pressed on. "Now, I know we've all had a few difficult evenings, but we must not let these recent, unconnected tragedies disrupt our lives. I'm not saying we should not be vigilant, but we cannot go on living with the belief that there are threats around every corner. These tragedies are the first of their kind in our town and should not define who we are. Instead of succumbing to our fears, I would ask that we all say a prayer for Sue Lawson's well-being. I have spoken with the emergency response team, and they have informed me that a helicopter will be landing here within the hour to medically evacuate her, so I need you to clear this area. That is all."

Before he walked away, ignoring the questions from the crowd, led by the ever so annoying, Jenny Maysure, Jay noted several hopeful looks and nods. He hoped he had done a better job of convincing them than he had himself.

***

Unable to believe what she had heard from Jay, Jenny returned to Barrens' Media more determined than ever to warn the people of Traders' Point about Dunn. The only trouble was that she would first need to convince her boss of that fact. When she entered his office, she was surprised to see a half-empty bottle of rum on Cody's desk. He quickly tucked it into a drawer, but he could not hide the evidence from his features.

"What can I do for you, Jenny?" Cody asked, slurring his words slightly.

Wishing she could step back out without him seeing her, Jenny sighed. "I think it's time that we revisit the decision not to run pieces on Maverick Dunn."

"Is that so?"

"Yes," Jenny said, trying to sound confident. "I think there's too much of a coincidence here to ignore, sir."

"Well," Cody said, staggering to his feet, "how's about you tell me what you've got?"

"Look at the facts," Jenny insisted. "This mysterious man arrives in town. He clearly has no roots anywhere. He also has access to a ridiculous amount of cash and a criminal record."

Cody stumbled over to her, close enough that she could smell his breath. "Lots of people have criminal records."

"True, but hear me out," Jenny pleaded. When he gestured for her to go on, she continued. "So, this mysterious man comes to town, and the first people he meets on his first night here are Kerry Giles, Dianne Smythe, and Hank Lawson."

"He also met you and your *fiancé*," Cody added.

She ignored this. "Then the man learns that people have started to look into who he is. He panics because he's on the run—"

"Allegedly."

"Allegedly," Jenny begrudgingly agreed. "But still. He begins to worry that something might come of it, so he disappears. Then, less than a week later, the first citizens of Traders' Point that he interacts with all die in mysterious circumstances."

Jenny was surprised when Cody simply shrugged. "That's pretty thin."

"You've got to be kidding me!" Jenny exploded.

"Don't forget who's in charge here," Cody warned.

"Boss, people are dying out there! Our friends and family could be next! I know Sheriff Chow is too lazy to protect us, but I would have thought that you would care more! What happens if he comes for you or—"

"That's it!" Cody shouted, cutting her off. "You're suspended until further notice! Now get the hell out of my building!"

Jenny recoiled as if she had been struck. She couldn't believe Cody was taking Sheriff Chow's side. She glared at him for a moment before grabbing her things and storming out.

***

Larry was surprised when his dad hollered to him from the kitchen that Jenny was at the door. They hadn't spoken to each other since the night she'd slapped him, and, in all honesty, Larry didn't know how to address the situation. He had hoped that Jenny would come over the following day to beg him for forgiveness, but she hadn't. In fact, Jenny had seemingly cut him off since then. He had begun to wonder if their relationship was over and had become depressed as a result. He eagerly got out of bed and made his way toward the kitchen.

"Don't let that woman beat you up again, son," Stan mocked.

Larry ignored the comment and opened the door. "Hi."

"Hi," Jenny said sheepishly. "Do you want to go for a walk?"

Larry nodded and stepped outside. The October storms had settled for the time being, and the sky was full of colours as the sun began to set. Larry saw Jenny shiver as the wind picked up, so he placed his jacket around her shoulders.

"Thanks," she said, not looking at him. She couldn't hide the tears that ran down her face though.

"Is everything okay?" Larry asked, his voice full of concern.

"I don't know anymore," Jenny said, her own voice trembling. "I feel like I'm losing everything."

He pulled her into his arms. "You still have me," he whispered.

She looked into his eyes for the first time. "Really?"

"Really. I love you, Jenny."

"I'm so sorry!" she said, burying her face in his chest. "I love you too."

"I know," he replied, hugging her tight.

They stayed that way for several moments, holding onto each other as if the world would crumble beneath them if they let go. She kissed him, fierce and passionate, and Larry knew their love was true. He silently scolded himself for having ever doubted her.

When she finally pulled away, a smile had replaced her tears. "Why don't you come over to my place, and I'll cook you an apology dinner?"

Larry grinned. "As if you have to ask."

***

Though she didn't know it, Jenny wasn't the only person in Traders' Point who hadn't been convinced by Sheriff Chow's speech that morning. Arthur and John Brusard had been two of the first to arrive at the fire the previous evening, and neither felt that it was possible for such an inferno to have simply been a tragic accident. Not wanting to tip off Sheriff Chow regarding their suspicions though, seeing as they were still serving as his deputies, the Brusard boys waited until long after nightfall before they made their way through the woodlands toward Hank's property. Even though they were certain that Sheriff Chow would be home with his family, he had permitted the hunters that had been staying with Hank and Sue to remain in their cabins until it was safe to travel by road out of the community. Neither of the Brusard boys wanted word of their investigation getting back to the sheriff unless they had something worth telling.

"Looks like the coast is clear," John whispered as they neared the burnt-out building.

"I told you Sheriff Chow would be too worried about maintaining peace to properly investigate this today," Art replied. "He hasn't even bothered to tape off the location."

John gestured to the rickety structure. "He likely just doesn't expect anybody would be crazy enough to try and go inside."

Art shrugged and pulled aside what remained of the back door, which Stan had kicked in during his rescue of Sue. He stepped inside, coughing immediately from the smell of fire and gas that still clung to the structure. Turning on a flashlight, John followed his brother's lead.

"Do you really think we'll find anything?" John asked.

Art turned and pointed back toward the door. "You tell me."

John shone his light toward the door and gasped. "Are those what I think they are?"

Art nodded. "Looks like old Hank popped off a round into the kitchen."

"I bet Sue wouldn't have been happy with that," John said, grinning.

Art sighed sadly. "I had really hoped that we would be wrong about this."

John's smile faded. "Let's just do what we came here to do."

Art pulled out a disposable camera and took a photo of the holes left by the shotgun blast. Then they made their way toward the living room. As the sheriff had suggested, it was obviously the place where the fire began. The ceiling had collapsed into the centre of the room, but much of the debris had been moved when Hank's body was retrieved. John shone his light at a spot on the floor a few feet away from them.

"What caliber do you think that is?" he asked.

Art walked over and took a closer look. "Seems likely that this was fired with a revolver."

"No shell casings," John agreed. "Think you can retrieve the bullet?"

"Probably best not to try," Art replied reluctantly before photographing the bullet hole.

"I don't see any gas canisters," John stated thoughtfully.

"Agreed," Art said, walking over to where Hank's chair had once been. "Help me lift this."

John set his light on a nearby table. Then, working together, they lifted a large piece of ceiling up and moved it out of the way. Even in the dim light, they could both see that was where the fire began. The flooring had fallen through to the ground and was charred to the point of crumbling when pressure was applied. John made an odd face as he bent down to retrieve something on the ground.

"What is it?" Art asked.

"I think it's a piece of rope," John replied, looking mortified.

Art lowered his head and nodded glumly. "I think the bastard lit Hank on fire."

With this revelation, John ran out of the burnt remnants of the building to throw up. Art took a few more photographs and then collected their things.

"Sorry, Hank," he said before stepping outside to join John.

Art found John still on his knees. He patted his younger brother on the back.

"This is fucking sick Art," John said as he stood up.

"I don't think it's over yet either."

"Then we need to put a stop to it!"

"How do you plan we do that?"

John pointed toward the ground in front of him. "I say we track this asshole drifter and even the score for Hank."

Art pointed the beam of the flashlight in the direction that John indicated. Even after all of the traffic in the area during the previous evening, a clear set of tracks led away from the structure and off into the forest. Art turned back to his brother, whose eyes gleamed with vengeance, and nodded. He turned off the light. The brothers checked to ensure their rifles were in working order and then they began to follow the tracks of the man they suspected of killing their fellow citizens.

After more than an hour of following his path through thick bushes and over difficult terrain, the tracks ended at a stream. Looking back toward the direction they came from, they discovered a second set of tracks and followed them for several minutes before discovering a revolver discarded in the bushes.

"What the hell is going on here, Art?" John asked, confused by what they had found.

"He went back, John," Art said, feeling fear grip him for the first time. "He's hiding somewhere in town."

After you were born, I had hoped that things would improve, but your mother's depression only seemed to get worse. She would rarely hold you, and she did not want to nurse you. She said that you reminded her of everything she hated about me. I tried to remain home to take care of you both myself, but my father insisted that I return to work. He hired a nanny to watch you while I was away. Every day that I left our home, I worried I would return to find one or both of you dead.

Marsha's brother was of little help. He worked odd jobs in the city, whenever he could actually find work, and never managed to hold a position for more than a month. In addition to this, he seemed to stop caring about helping his sister and would instead spend his nights drinking himself into a stupor in our spare bedroom. I had hoped his presence would improve my relationship with your mother. Instead, his behaviour became a source of many arguments between us.

About ten months after you were born, I thought I had finally found a way to restore your mother back to the woman I had fallen in love with. I suddenly realized that one of my father's lessons was the key to doing so. What I needed to do was find a way to motivate her. Knowing that she had grown up with so little, it did not surprise me that she had desired more from life. She also reminded me daily now that, were it not for my wealth and status, she would have left long ago. So, I thought an opportunity to create a name for herself might be the key to giving her a chance to create for herself the happiness that I had failed to provide her. Perhaps then she might even improve enough to be the loving mother that I knew she could be. At that precise moment, it just so happened that my father's company had such an opportunity available. All I needed to do was talk both of them into it.

CHAPTER 11

October 15, 2011

Ike couldn't sleep. Though he was physically exhausted from his efforts to save Sue the previous day, his mind kept replaying the events of the fire. He had been all but useless until Stan had pulled Sue from the fire, and he felt guilty about it. It also did not help that, whenever Ike did manage to fall asleep, his dreams were haunted by the images of the dead. They would come to him and accuse him of failing to save them. They would blame him for not doing enough to find the killer and stop him from claiming more victims. Ike would wake up to find himself drenched in sweat whenever the nightmares occurred.

Ike felt compelled to redeem himself. He made a large thermos of coffee, grabbed a fresh pack of smokes, and descended into the basement. The smell of burnt flesh hit him partway down the stairs, and Ike nearly threw up over the side of the banister. Taking a moment to regain his composure, Ike considered going back up to bed and dealing with this later. Then the taunting voices from his nightmares crept back into his thoughts, and he became more determined than ever to find some clue that would prove that a killer was stalking the citizens of Traders' Point. He covered his mouth with a scarf and then walked over to the slab where Hank's body lay. Ike set down his coffee and lit a cigarette. The fresh wave of nicotine rapidly settled his nerves. Ike washed up and set to work upon his task.

It wasn't long before Ike found the bullet wound in Hank's thigh. He carefully extracted the bullet and set it off to the side for the sheriff. Within an hour, Ike had learned that Hank had also suffered a significant wound on the back of his head. Surely these would be enough proof that the fire that claimed Hank's life was anything but an accident. Satisfied with his work, Ike lit another smoke and began working on his notes.

Ike paused when he thought he heard the creak of footsteps above his head. Checking his watch, Ike was surprised to see that it was only 4:00 a.m. Brittany wasn't expected to arrive for several hours yet, but perhaps she was being plagued by the same fears and nightmares he was. Thinking she must have let herself into his home, Ike set down his pen and put out his cigarette. If the girl was traumatized by everything that had happened recently, he would not be surprised. As her uncle and her boss, he felt compelled to try and set her mind at ease, especially given the pregnancy. He walked up the stairs and opened the basement door. Before him stood a man dressed in black from head to toe. Before Ike could do anything, the man shoved him back into the basement. Ike fell backwards, clearing the small staircase, and struck his head on the cement floor below. He tried to move but found he was unable to. He heard the man coming down the stairs and tried to scream for help, but he could only utter a guttural sound of pain.

"Sorry, Doc," a familiar voice said. "I don't have a choice."

Before Ike could respond, two large hands seized him by the head and snapped his neck.

***

"Shit," Jenny muttered as she approached Dr. Sindell's office. She had hoped to slip into the office unnoticed, so she could catch the good doctor off guard as she had before, but that plan was ruined when she saw Brittany Kyle pacing around frantically outside. Jenny had barely gotten out of her vehicle before the girl was upon her.

"Have you seen my uncle this morning?" she asked desperately.

"I'm afraid not," Jenny replied. "In fact, I doubt he was expecting me."

"Is that because you were suspended?" Brittany asked with a grin, momentarily forgetting her distress.

Jenny tapped a finger to her nose. "I guess word travels fast. I was hoping to convince your uncle to help me write a compassionate piece about the fire, so I could get back into Mr. Barrens' good graces. So, what are you doing standing out here in the rain?"

The panic instantly returned to the girl's eyes. "The office is locked."

Jenny tried to sound reassuring. "I'm sure your uncle is just sleeping."

"No," Brittany declared. "Dr. Sindell is a professional. He would never want to keep his patients waiting. Something is seriously wrong."

"Did you try the door around back?"

Brittany nodded. "And there's a light on in the basement."

"Okay. Can you keep a secret?"

"Yes."

"Let's go around back then, and I'll pick the lock."

Brittany looked mortified. "You know how to do that?"

Jenny grinned. "You learn to do a lot of things if you want to be a good journalist. I need you to keep an eye out for anybody passing by while I do this though. It isn't exactly legal."

Brittany nodded and then Jenny disappeared around the back. A few minutes later the two women were entering the building. The narrow hallway was dark, so Jenny pulled out a flashlight and turned it on. Nothing appeared to be out of the ordinary.

"You said you saw a light on in the basement?" Jenny asked.

"Yeah. There's a door up ahead that joins the office to his house," Brittany whispered. "He turned it into a morgue after Kerry Giles was killed to keep the bodies from spoiling. He wants to make sure they still look good when we can finally have some proper funerals."

Jenny smiled. She had always admired the simple yet caring way in which Dr. Sindell approached his practice. They crept through the office and made their way toward the small home that was attached to it. They passed through the door, which was unlocked. Jenny kept an eye out for any signs of a disturbance having taken place. Her attention to detail had always benefitted her, and she was glad not to see anything out of place. It gave her hope that Brittany had panicked for nothing. However, that hope vanished when they came upon the open basement door.

"Uncle Ike!" Brittany screamed and then ran down the stairs.

Jenny tore after her and grabbed her arm before she could reach the bottom.

"Don't touch anything!" she commanded.

"But he might still be alive!" Brittany begged.

It killed Jenny to say it, but she knew a lifeless body when she saw one. "No, Brittany, he's gone."

The mournful wails of the girl who clung to Jenny were enough to make the most stone-hearted of men cry. Not even the thunderstorm raging outside could drown them out.

***

The police station erupted with the voices of the outraged citizens of Traders' Point. Despite Jay's efforts to keep Ike's death quiet, word had spread like wildfire. Now Jay's greatest fears for his people were coming true. The town was falling apart at the seams, and the constant storms kept the vacationing hunters trapped with them as well. Nobody knew who to trust, including him, and they were all demanding that he fix the problem.

"Enough is enough!" Stan growled.

"How many more people does this sack of shit have to kill?" an out-of-town hunter asked.

"Look," Jay said, trying to be patient, "Dr. Sindell's death appears to be a tragic—"

"Accident!" Mrs. Kyle, Ike's wealthy sister, screamed. "How dare you?"

"I'm sorry, Mrs. Kyle, but—"

She jabbed a wrinkled finger weighted down by several rings into Jay's chest. "Don't you 'but' me, young man! My brother was murdered just like all the rest, and it is high time that you do something to protect us! If you can't stop him, then maybe we should find someone who can!"

A roar of approval rose from the mob. Jay was losing them and feared they were going to start a riot. He began to panic.

"Please listen to me!" he shouted. "I know that you're all scared, but there is simply no evidence—"

"You want evidence?" Arthur Brusard shouted from near the back of the crowd.

The people parted for the Brusard boys to step forward. John slammed a series of photographs onto Jay's desk, and Art laid the revolver down on top of them.

"What are these?" Jay asked, fearing he already knew the answer.

"We took a trip out to Hank' place last night," Art replied. "Did you know that he was shot before the fire was started?"

A mixture of fearful and angry cries rose from the townsfolk. Jay tried to ignore them. "What makes you think this weapon belongs to the killer?" he asked cautiously.

"I sold it to the drifter," Art replied. "I know my product, Sheriff."

"How did you come to possess it?" Jay asked through clenched teeth.

"He dropped it in the woods!" John exclaimed. "On his way back to town!"

Now the voices all held varying degrees of panic. Jay froze in place, realizing that Jenny had been right all along. His thoughts were drowned out by the crowd.

"When will you admit that we're in danger?"

"How are you going to stop the killer?"

"Are we even safe in our homes?"

"We should organize a party to hunt the bastard down!"

This last cry came from Stan, and it was met with a loud round of applause. Jay's fears shifted in that moment from concern that the townsfolk would turn on themselves to the idea that they might be playing right into the killer's hands.

"Settle down!" he bellowed. "I'm in charge here, and I'll not have vigilantes taking the law into their own hands! Any man caught in the woods with a weapon will find himself sitting behind bars with Kennedy Smythe! Are we clear?"

Most of the voices died down, but Mrs. Kyle was not going to be convinced so easily. "Would you have us wait to be picked off like animals in our own homes?"

"No!" Jay retorted, then lowered his voice. "No. I admit that I was wrong about this. There's a threat in our forest, and we need to look out for each other. I'll reach out to the FBI and ask for the support we need to take this menace down. Until then I am declaring the woodlands off limits. Also, since this bastard only seems to hunt in the dark, I am placing a curfew on Traders' Point. Nobody is to be out of their homes after sunset. Finally, since the FBI will surely be delayed by the storms, I am establishing a round-the-clock guard to patrol the community. I'll contact those whom I'll be recruiting for this task later today. Now return to your homes, and listen to the radio for further updates."

Though they were reluctant, the crowd complied. When they were gone, Jay turned back to his desk to retrieve a bottle. He needed a stiff drink now more than ever. A voice from the corner made him choke on his first swig as his glass shattered on the floor.

"Do you really believe that the drifter is your killer, Sheriff?" Cody asked solemnly.

"I honestly don't know any more," Jay admitted. "But you'd better get your girl to come into my office in the morning. I'm going to need to know everything that she has learned about Maverick Dunn. If he is the killer, she might be the only person in town who knows how to stop the son of a bitch."

Cody nodded and then turned to leave.

"I'm sorry for squashing your story," Jay said through his tears.

"So am I," Cody replied.

Things at Heis Footwear had been improving steadily over the past year, and I thought we were ready to compete at a national level. I had convinced my father that it would be in our best interest to expand our market. To do this successfully, I stressed to my father that it would be essential for us to put out an advertisement on television. I was even fairly certain that I could make such a commercial for minimal cost, as a friend who owed me a favour from college had recently opened a film production company. My father was impressed by my commitment to our family and agreed wholeheartedly with my idea.

Of course, my real motivations were of a more personal nature. Without realizing it, my father had signed a contract that would allow Marsha to participate in the commercial as an actress. I knew it wasn't much, but I hoped she would see it as a chance to do something for herself. Perhaps if she were to gain some self-confidence, it might be enough to snap her out of her depression. I know it was a foolish hope, but it was all I had.

I was pleasantly surprised when she agreed to participate without a fight. Marsha readily prepared for her part and, even though it was just a few lines, spent hours rehearsing with me. The part turned out to be even more of a miracle than I had hoped for. My friend said your mother had real talent and recruited her for a few other commercials that he was shooting in the area over the next couple of months. Marsha loved the experience and told me that she believed she had found her calling. She finally seemed to be happy at home. She was spending time with you, and she was spending time with me. We had even talked about planning a trip for our anniversary. I thought all of this meant that she was finally ready to commit to living our lives together. I could not have been more wrong.

CHAPTER 12

October 16, 2011

Jenny stood outside of the police station trying to calm herself before she entered. At the moment, she wasn't sure if she was more anguished at the senseless loss of life or pissed off about what she'd learned from Cody on the phone that morning. Her boss had called to lift her suspension and inform her that Sheriff Chow was asking for her help. At first Jenny had to admit she felt a bit smug about the man's sudden change of heart. However, when Cody explained that he had agreed to go along with Sheriff Chow's plan to get a buddy at the FBI to bury the outstanding warrant for Maverick Dunn in an effort to maintain peace in Traders' Point, Jenny had broken the coffee pot on the counter. Jenny had been right all along about the threat that Dunn had posed, and if the fools had listened to her sooner, Dianne, Hank, and Ike would still be alive. Even though this was true, Jenny knew that neither gloating nor screaming at Sheriff Chow would get their community out of the situation that they now found themselves in. Jenny took one more deep breath and then stepped inside.

Jay stood up from his desk. "Can I get you any coffee?"

"Cut the crap," Jenny snapped. "Just tell me what you need."

"Fine," he replied with a shrug. "To start things off, I need to know who else might be a target for this drifter of yours."

"You mean Maverick Dunn?" Jenny asked bitterly.

"Yes," Jay replied with disdain. "Can we just get past the part where you rub in my face how badly I fucked this up and get to the part where you help me save those of us who are still left? We both know that's the only reason you came here."

"Fair enough," Jenny replied. "Dunn seems to be targeting everyone that he had an interaction with during the few days that he was seen in town."

Jay began jotting down notes. "Care to guess why he's doing it?"

Jenny sighed. "I think we might both be responsible for that."

Jay's face fell. "You're saying we put too much pressure on him?"

Jenny nodded. "The man was clearly on a mission. I figure he didn't want to take the chance that he might end up behind bars again, so he disappeared into the forest and then began to eliminate any witnesses who could place him here."

"What exactly is his mission?"

"He's searching for a man with the last name 'Heis.'"

"I get that," Jay said, looking perplexed, "but if his file at the FBI is correct, then he has already killed the man who framed him. So, who's he looking for?"

"I think he's trying to find the son of Albert Heis. The one who was married to his sister."

"You think he wants to kill off the entire family line?"

"Exactly," Jenny replied.

"Okay, so who else had contact with him in town?"

Jenny pulled out her notes. "He visited Hirsch General Store to speak to Larry after the incident in the Diner, he purchased goods from the Brusard boys, and he stopped by Barrens' Media to try and look up some information."

"Shit," Jay muttered. "Who knows how many people he spoke to while visiting all of those locations. There are too many targets to properly protect everyone."

"What are you going to do then?" Jenny asked, more worried than angry for the first time that day.

"We have no choice but to maintain general patrols and hope the storms will break long enough for the road to become accessible again," Jay said, placing his face into his hands.

Jenny thought about saying something else but didn't know how to comfort him. There was no way that she was willing to absolve him of his guilt. She also had no clue how to motivate him without doing so. Jenny set her files down on his desk and walked out of the building followed by the echo of Jay's sobs.

***

Mary slowly made her way toward the Hirsch General Store. Though she had made up her mind to go through with this confrontation, she still felt incredibly nervous. The recent deaths in the community were clearly all related in some way, and, based on what her daughter had shared of her research, it all tied back to Stan and Larry Hirsch. Since Larry had lived there nearly his entire life, Mary doubted he had anything to do with what was going on. However, the same could not be said of his father.

Stan had arrived in Traders' Point under the cover of darkness late one evening in the fall of 1988. When he arrived at their door, a storm was raging very similar to the one they were experiencing now, and he was soaked through to the bone. He said he had only a backpack filled with a few belongings and some clothes. He was also holding a baby in his arms. The man was clearly weak with fever, but even so, Mary's husband had been wary of letting him in. However, Mary could not say no to the child. She convinced her husband to let them stay for a few days to recover. It was the least they could do.

It was nearly a week before the man's fever broke. Even after that the only thing he could share at first was that his name was Stan, and his boy was named Larry. When pressed for more information, Stan would become delirious as a result of the effort to concentrate on a response. Though she objected, Mary's husband insisted that they fix him up with a room somewhere else, so Mary had convinced Abel Hirsch to take him in. She figured that the old man could use the extra help stocking shelves, since he had recently been diagnosed with cancer, and it would give the child a roof and some food. Over the next several weeks, Stan's memory had slowly returned. She learned that he had actually come to Traders' Point precisely because he had heard of his great uncle's condition. At the time it seemed odd to her, as Abel had never mentioned any relatives. However, with time Mary had forgotten about this story, as she suspected everyone else who lived there at the time had.

However, recent events had pulled these memories back out of the deepest corners of her mind. They had been nagging Mary during her days and disturbing her dreams at night. Now she could no longer withstand her curiosity. Though she feared what it might do to her daughter's relationship with Larry, Mary needed to know if the chaos that had befallen her hometown was the fault of the man she had once saved. Mary took a deep breath and then stepped into the store.

"Good morning, Mrs. Maysure," Stan said pleasantly. "What can I help you with today?"

"I'm afraid my daughter broke our coffee pot this morning," Mary replied, matching his tone. "I don't suppose you have a spare?"

"There could be one in the back," Stan said, scratching his head. "Larry, go check in the back for your future mother-in-law, would you?"

Larry set down a case filled with cartons of eggs and headed toward the back room. Mary waited until she was sure he was out of earshot before stepping up to the counter. "Do you remember the night that I saved your life?" she whispered.

All of the cheer left him in an instant. "I'd rather we not discuss this where Larry might hear us."

"I need to know," Mary insisted. "Does this killer have something to do with your past, Stan?"

He gave her a hard look, but Mary refused to break eye contact. Finally, he shrugged. "I have no idea who this guy thinks I am, but I swear I've never seen him before, okay?"

Before she could say anything more on the matter, Larry returned with the coffee pot. "I'm afraid it's a bit dirty from storage," he said shyly.

"It's perfect, dear," Mary said, taking the pot.

Stan rang up her purchase, and Mary paid him. Then she bid them both farewell in the same cheerful tone she had feigned earlier and left the store, confident that she had everything that she needed.

***

The Brusard boys had spent their day restocking and tidying up the store. With the sheriff's ban on entering the forest, there was little point in opening up. So, they were both startled when a loud knock came on their front door. John walked over, pistol in hand, to see who it was.

"Holy crap, John!" Stan exclaimed through the door. "Are you selling the guns or threatening your customers with them?"

"Sorry Stan," John muttered. "Store is closed today."

"Yeah, I saw the sign," Stan replied. "I just hoped you might make an exception for a local."

John looked at his older brother for approval, and Art nodded, so John stepped aside to let Stan come in.

"You need to make this quick, Stan," Art said. "Sheriff Chow has asked us to be on patrol for the first of the evening shifts."

"Well, at least he's finally doing something about the killer," Stan replied. "I'm here to buy a revolver."

"Something wrong with yours?" John asked impulsively.

Art shot him a disappointing glance, but Stan just waved off the comment. "Actually, it began to misfire quite some time ago. Figured it was still intimidating enough on its own to make robbers think twice about trying to steal from me before. But now..."

"You can't take any chances," John said, finishing his thought.

"Exactly," Stan replied. "So, have you got anything in stock?"

John showed him several models, and Stan picked out a Colt. John handed him a box of ammo for it, and Art rang him up.

"Stay safe," Art said as he handed Stan his change.

"You too," Stan replied. "Be sure to watch each other's backs out there."

It was a few days before your first birthday. I was running late, and I had barely made it to the bakery in time to pick up your cake. It was a vanilla cherry chip in the shape of a race car with cream cheese frosting. I realized the toy store would be closed, so I decided to head home with the cake and a promise to stop for your gift on my lunch hour the following day. I hoped your mother wouldn't be too upset. It was around 7:00 p.m. when I pulled into the driveway. As I hurried inside, I failed to see your mother's luggage, which I tripped over, spilling your cake on the tile floor. Cursing, I called to your mother. She emerged from the upstairs bedroom with a sigh and told me that she had hoped to be gone before I returned. She explained that she was leaving our family and driving to LA to become a full-time actress. The argument that followed was the worst that we ever had. It led to a revelation that would change everything. I could not have imagined the secret that your mother had been keeping from me. A secret that would ruin all of our lives.

CHAPTER 13

October 17, 2011

Mary sat in her rocking chair sipping a glass of tea while Larry and Jenny sat on the small plaid couch by the radio, listening intently to Sheriff Chow's morning announcement.

"Citizens of Traders' Point, I'm afraid I have a mixed bag of news for you this morning. As the thunderstorms have continued on and off throughout the evening, the roads remain unpassable. I'm afraid it will be at least one more day before we receive assistance from the FBI. Therefore, the community lockdown of the forest and curfew after sunset will remain in place until further notice.

"On a more positive note, the community patrols seem to be working. After a quick series of house calls this morning, I can declare confidently that there were no attacks by the killer during the previous evening. If we continue to be vigilant and follow the protocols that are in place, we can get through this. That's all for now. Stay safe, everybody."

Jenny scoffed. "He actually sounds like he's proud that nobody was killed."

"Don't be so quick to judge," Mary chided. "I'm sure he's doing the best that he can."

"Now," Larry remarked sarcastically.

"He should have listened to me when I first brought Dunn to his attention," Jenny added.

Mary raised her hands in surrender. "I'm not arguing with either of you. I'm just saying that being in charge means having a lot of pressure on your shoulders."

Jenny sighed. "I suppose so."

Larry shook his head. "Too many people have died without any justice."

"Those are your father's words, Larry Hirsch," Mary said with all of the authority of a parent who was disappointed in her child. "There will be no talk of vengeance in this house. Do you understand?"

"Yes, ma'am," Larry replied solemnly.

"Are you going to open the shop today, Mother?" Jenny asked. It was an obvious attempt to switch the subject, and Mary thought about scolding her as well, but held back.

"Perhaps for the morning, but I'm running low on several of my herbs."

"You're not thinking of going into the forest?" Jenny asked, her voice full of concern.

"The sheriff just said that the lockdown is still in place," Larry added.

"Yes, I know," Mary said, "but I'll not be told when I can and cannot enter my own woods. I've been picking from these forests since before either of you were born. I won't be intimidated out of doing it now."

"Didn't you go out into the forest a couple of weeks ago though?" Jenny asked desperately. "Surely you can wait a few more days."

"Yes, I know I went out recently," Mary replied hastily, "but there has been a higher demand for cold remedies this month, and I need to restock now, or I won't be able to complete my orders before the mail goes out."

"Perhaps we can go with you then," Larry suggested.

"Nonsense," Mary replied dismissively.

"Well, at least take somebody with you," Jenny begged. "Perhaps one of the Brusard boys?"

"The sheriff has warned us against travelling alone," Larry added.

"Alright," Mary said with a sigh, seeing there would be no end to this otherwise. "I'll ask Arthur Brusard to go with me. Satisfied?"

They nodded in unison.

"Good," Mary said. "Now, what about the two of you?"

"We plan on staying right here with you today," Jenny said.

"Oh no you don't," Mary scolded. "You're not going to treat me like a fragile vase, young lady."

"But Mrs. Maysure..." Larry began.

"That's enough," Mary said. "I'm perfectly capable of taking care of myself. Now the two of you are going to go over to your father's house tonight, Larry, and make sure he eats a good meal. We all know Hirsch men are lousy cooks, and I won't have him eating canned soup and crackers for the duration of this lockdown."

The lovers hung their heads in defeat but nodded in acknowledgement. Satisfied, Mary returned to sipping her tea and enjoying the soft music that complemented the silence that followed.

***

Mary knew it was only a matter of time before Jenny would be compelled to go into the office and do some work. Although Jenny was clearly afraid for her mother's safety, she was too driven to succeed to sit around the house all day listening to the radio. Jenny took after her father in that regard and, combined with the curiosity that she'd inherited from Mary, there was no way that Jenny could resist the call of a hot story. Fortunately for Mary, Jenny dragged Larry along for the trip.

Mary waited until she was certain they were gone before putting her plan into action. She changed into a pair of earth-tone hiking pants and a warm, beige sweatshirt. She pulled on a pair of thick socks and put on her hiking boots. Mary completed the outfit with an evergreen-coloured cloak and hood. Then, taking up her large walking stick, she headed out her door.

Knowing that Sheriff Chow was serious about his ban on entering the forest, Mary made sure that she could blend in with the foliage. She had chosen her outfit in such a way that, if she were to stand perfectly still, only a person with a very keen eye would be able to pick her out from amongst the trees. Mary had to complete her quest without anybody knowing she was involved. After all, if she failed, it could mean her life and possibly Jenny's as well. Mary slipped into the trees behind her house and disappeared from view.

It took more than an hour to hike around the sheriff's patrols. There were several instances when somebody caught a glimpse of her moving about. However, Mary would freeze in place and wait until the person who had spotted her dismissed her as an animal or an optical illusion. Finally, she reached her goal, arriving at a small cabin tucked into the woods outside of town. Mary crouched just inside the treeline, trying to decide how to get his attention, when Arthur Brusard stepped out. She tossed a small rock in his direction and waved when he turned to face her. Art grabbed his rifle and walked over to meet her.

"Are you sure you want to do it this way?" he asked, looking a bit uncertain.

"Definitely," Mary replied confidently. "If I'm wrong about this, the last thing I want to do is embarrass anybody with false accusations."

Arthur looked over his shoulder. "Well, at least let me invite John along. It can't hurt to have an extra gun for something like this."

Mary shook her head. "Sheriff Chow will find it odd if one of you is late for your watch. If you're both missing, he might panic and try looking for you."

Arthur begrudgingly agreed, and they walked into the forest together.

***

Larry sat in the newsroom of Barrens' Media impatiently tapping his foot on the floor. Although he wasn't surprised by Jenny's dedication to her job, he did not enjoy having to wait for her. Especially when "Thirty minutes, tops" had turned into more than two hours. He had read the current paper twice as well as the previous three issues. Larry really wanted to get going to his place before his dad decided to cook something for himself again. However, he knew better than to disturb Jenny while she was in her office. So, he just continued to sit, humming along with the tunes that poured out of the radio.

After another twenty minutes or so had passed, Jenny finally stepped out of her office. Larry stood, but she waved him off dismissively, and he returned to his seat. She darted into Cody's office and spoke to him for a few minutes. When she re-emerged, she greeted Larry with a smile and a kiss on the lips.

"Sorry to keep you waiting, darling," Jenny said with a hint of regret.

"It's okay," Larry replied, smiling. "Let's just get going."

Jenny looked at the clock on the wall and chuckled. "I guess we'd better hurry if we don't want to eat tomato soup and grilled cheese sandwiches."

"I wouldn't laugh," Larry said, feigning horror. "Charred sandwiches have been known to make people choke."

Jenny rolled her eyes and punched him playfully. As they stepped outside, they instantly became aware of the dramatic changes in the weather that had taken place. A light drizzle, with the sun peeking through the clouds to warm things up a bit, had been replaced with a torrential storm with howling winds that chilled them to the bone. Regretting their decision to leave Jenny's car at her mom's place, they ran to Larry's home. They burst through the back door, tumbling to the floor and laughing, startling Stan.

"What the hell are you doing out in this?" Stan hollered as he walked over to slam the door.

"Sorry, Mr. Hirsch," Jenny replied timidly. "I lost track of time at work and—"

"No," Stan interrupted, a stern expression on his face. "I mean why are you coming over here? I thought you would be at your mother's place again."

Larry stood up and helped Jenny to her feet. "Mrs. Maysure thought we should come over and make sure you had a hearty meal for a change."

Stan's features morphed from anger to fear. "You shouldn't be here. Who will protect Mary if you're here?"

"My mother will be fine," Jenny said confidently. "She's become very independent since my father died."

Larry nodded in agreement. "She even went out into the forest to collect some more herbs for her store this afternoon."

Stan's face turned a deep shade of red. "No!" he exclaimed before running out of the room.

"What's going on?" Jenny whispered.

Before Larry could reply, Stan returned to the kitchen with his rifle slung over his shoulder and a revolver tucked into his belt. "I'm going out!"

"Are you crazy?" Jenny shouted.

Larry stepped between his dad and the door. "I'm sure Mrs. Maysure is fine, Dad. Why don't we just calls"

"Out of my way!" Stan screamed, shoving Larry to the ground. "I'm putting an end to this tonight!"

With that he ran out the door and disappeared into the storm, leaving Larry and Jenny frightened and huddled together on the kitchen floor.

***

It had taken several hours longer than normal to hike to the clearing tucked deep into the forest, but they had to do so carefully. Art and Mary had no way of knowing whether or not the killer was in the woods, and they did not wish to alert him to their presence. In addition, the storm had picked up dramatically, making the terrain muddy and difficult to navigate. Although Art was certain that the clearing was straight ahead, the absolute darkness made it impossible to determine if it was actually safe to leave the treeline.

"Are you sure this is where you saw the pit?" Art asked, feeling slightly unnerved.

"Positive," Mary said. "I came across it several days ago."

"What makes you think the drifter is down there?"

"Honestly, it's just a hunch," Mary replied, blushing. "I really hope I'm wrong about this, Arthur."

"Same here," he replied, checking his weapon. "Alright, I'm going to crawl toward the pit and check inside. You stay here and keep hidden in case there's trouble."

"I should come with you," Mary said, grabbing his arm. "The killer could be out there right now."

"That's why I need you to remain here," Art said. "If something happens, your best chance at getting help is to have a head start."

"You can't honestly expect me to leave you behind."

"You have to, Mary," Art insisted. "This has to end tonight. Take this walkie-talkie, and call John if there's any trouble. Then run and don't look back."

Art could see the pain in her eyes, but she nodded in agreement. He began to combat crawl toward the pit in the centre of the clearing. The low rumble of thunder around him felt foreboding, but if Mary was right, the only proof might be lying at the bottom of that hole. He was glad for the rain, hoping it would mask the sound of his movements. As he neared the pit though, a familiar voice began to call out bitterly.

"Heis!" Dunn bellowed. "You coward!"

Afraid the man would give away his position, Art rose to his feet and ran the last few yards over to the pit. At that moment, a bolt of lightning lit up the sky, and Art could make out the man trapped below. The bottom of the pit was lined with jagged rocks, and the man had clearly been injured in the fall. Arthur feared for a moment that this rescue might be for nothing after all, should the man be unable to escape the pit. Art wished then that he had asked John to come along.

"Dunn?" Art called down in a hushed tone.

"Thank God," Dunn replied. "I thought I was going to die in this stupid fucking hole."

"Can you move?"

"Yeah, I think I only broke my right leg. It's pretty messed up though."

"That's good," Art replied. "I'm going to lower a rope, so you can climb up."

"I don't think you'll be able to support my weight," Dunn said. "Is there anything that you can anchor the rope to?"

"Let me worry about that," Arthur replied. "We need to get out of here now."

"Let's do it then."

Arthur set his rifle down and untied a large length of rope from around his waist. Fastening one end of the rope to his belt, he wrapped it around his arm a few times and then tossed the remainder of it down the hole. Arthur heard Dunn crawling over to where the rope had landed and then felt the pull as he began his ascent. Arthur dug his heels into the mud, trying not to be tugged down into the pit as Dunn grunted and pulled his way up to the surface. When another flash of lightning revealed a massive hand extending out of the pit, Arthur grabbed hold and pulled Dunn up to the top. They lay in the grass, both of them breathing heavily.

"Thanks," Dunn gasped. "Thought I would never get to touch grass again."

"We're not out of this yet," Art stated as he helped Dunn to his feet. "Not until you get back to town."

"You're not going anywhere!" a voice boomed in the darkness.

Another flash of lightning lit up the sky, revealing Stan Hirsch standing just inside the clearing, his rifle raised for the kill shot. Art's rifle lay a few paces away from Dunn. He made a slight motion to Dunn to indicate its position. Then Art released him and stood up to face his enemy.

"So, it's true then," Art said, hoping to attract Stan's focus to him.

"You weren't supposed to be here, Arthur!" Stan shouted.

"I suppose not," Art said, taking a step away from Dunn. "I imagine you had hoped to kill my brother and me at the same time."

"Stop moving, you son of a bitch!" Stan commanded, firing a shot in Art's direction.

"Is this really how it's going to be?" Art asked, taking another step. "I've known you since I was a child. Can you really kill me, Stan?"

"I don't have a choice!" Stan shouted. "My son can't know what happened!"

The sky was lit up once more by the flash of lightning. In that instant a series of events unfolded. Stan saw both men clearly as Dunn seized hold of Art's rifle. Stan turned his sights to the wounded man, but Dunn was faster. Both men managed to fire off a round at the same time. Stan appeared to be struck in the right shoulder, the force of the impact sending him falling backwards to the ground. Stan's shot was luckier though. It had struck Dunn through the throat. Art ran over to the man, but a bullet shattered his left knee before he could reach him. Stan struggled back to his feet and began to approach where Dunn had fallen. Art heard him reloading and knew that he had only one chance. He crawled desperately toward his own gun, but a second shot hit him in the spine before he could reach it.

"It didn't have to be this way!" Stan shouted as he stood over his victims.

"Fuck you, Stan!" Art shouted, spitting blood at him.

"Fitting last words," Stan replied, raising his rifle for the final blow.

A beam of light suddenly shot across the clearing, blinding Stan. He fired a shot, narrowly missing Arthur. With all of his remaining strength, Arthur lunged forward and tackled Stan to the ground.

"Run!" he shouted as Stan struggled to free himself.

The bushes where Mary had been hiding rustled violently as she fled. Stan kicked Art in the ribs and grabbed his rifle. He fired two shots in her direction before Art could bring him down once more. They wrestled over the weapon for a few moments, but Stan was clearly stronger.

"Fuck you!" he shouted, striking Art in the face with his rifle. "Who the hell is out there?"

"It's too late," Art said with a chuckle, spitting up more blood. "You'll never be able to stop her now."

"Fuck!" Stan screamed, tossing his empty rifle aside.

Art silently prayed for Mary to survive as he heard Stan cock his revolver.

As soon as the words left her lips, I could see the hurt and regret in her eyes. It was too late though. Nothing would ever be the same. Even as I silently prayed to God that it wasn't true, I knew there was no denying that it was. My father had raped your mother. It had happened once, before our marriage, and several more times after we returned from our honeymoon. She also told me that you were his child. Suddenly, it all made sense. The hatred she held for my family. The way she recoiled at my touch. The fact that she wanted so little to do with you when you were born. The reason she wanted to be rid of you before that could ever occur. It hit me all at once as I stood frozen in the tumultuous storm of emotions raging in my heart and thoughts of malice in my head.

To her credit, Marsha tried to wait for me to come to grips with my new reality. She placed a hand gently on my arm, and I could see the infinite sadness in her eyes. She told me it was over. She could not bear to live with us any longer. She needed to find some sort of meaning to all of this, and she needed to do it without any reminders of what had happened to her. She said she needed to make something of her life.

She kissed me on the cheek and tried to take hold of her bags, but I grabbed her by the wrist. I wanted to accept her words as truth, to give her a chance to live free from her torment, but I couldn't. I also couldn't let her leave us. Not now. Not without giving me a chance to make everything better. She tried to pull away and yelled at me, but I wouldn't let her go. When she slapped me, I lost what little control I had left over my senses. I swung her into the wall with tremendous force. Her head struck an antique mirror, and she began to bleed. Seeing this, I let go of her wrist, and she collapsed to the floor.

Feeling ashamed, I tried to apologize, but Marsha would have none of it. She cursed me and my entire family. She said I was no better than my father and that I deserved all of the misery that he brought on me because I wasn't man enough to stand up to him. She called me a coward and told me she'd hated me ever since I left her behind to go to college. She said she'd just used me and that I was no longer needed.

My rage overtook my reason. I can only recall flashes of what happened next. I remember grabbing the metal baseball bat by the door, the sound of flesh being crushed beneath the force of my blows, and the warm spray of mist on my face as I struck her. Then I blacked out.

CHAPTER 15

October 18, 2011

If Jenny had been frightened when Stan had stormed out, she was terrified when, upon returning with Larry to her own home, she discovered that her mother was still out. Jenny wanted to run off into the storm right then, but Larry had talked her out of it.

"Maybe she went to stay with a friend," he suggested.

"She would have left me a note," Jenny replied. "What if the killer has done something to her?"

Larry's face became solemn. "Even if that were the case, there isn't anything that we can do now."

"We can go out there! We can search the woods! We have to find her!" Jenny began to sob.

Larry embraced her, but he refused to relent. "If we go out there, we would only be making ourselves a target in this storm as well. We need to trust that your mom can take care of herself."

Jenny had been reluctant to agree, but she saw no point in arguing. Instead she allowed him to dote over her, preparing a meal that was barely edible and going to the bedroom to lie down. Larry had probably hoped to get her to fall asleep, but he was the only one who did. Jenny could only lie there imagining all manner of horrors that her mother might be experiencing at that moment. She prayed to whatever god might be listening that her desire for a story would not be the catalyst that took her mother from her.

A loud crash made Jenny jump so badly that Larry fell out of bed.

"What's going on?" he asked groggily.

"Hush," Jenny replied. "I think somebody is in the house."

They crept to the bedroom door and cracked it open. From out of the darkness, two distinct voices could be heard.

"Please don't do this!" Mary begged.

"What choice do I have?" Stan yelled. "He can't know the truth!"

"I don't even know what the truth is!" Mary cried.

"That doesn't matter now! You should have never gotten involved, Mary!"

"Dad!" Larry shouted, pushing past Jenny and running out of the room.

Jenny followed Larry to the kitchen and froze in fear beside him. Her mother was lying on the floor, crouching against the oven in the fetal position, begging for her life. Stan was standing in the inner doorway, his eyes full of hate and a revolver aimed at her head.

"What are you doing here, boy?" Stan yelled, refusing to look away from Mary.

"What am I doing?" Larry shouted back. "What the hell are you doing?"

"I'm putting an end to all of this, son," Stan replied solemnly.

"Please don't shoot my mom, Mr. Hirsch," Jenny begged.

Fury blazed in Stan's eyes as he turned to face her. "You! This is all because of you! I told you not to look into who the fucking drifter was, but you just couldn't let it go!"

Stan pointed the gun at Jenny, but Larry stepped between them before he could fire.

"I won't let you hurt her!" he shouted.

Stan's hand shook as tears began to pour from his eyes. "I didn't want this for you, son. I didn't want any of this. I tried to take you away from it all. I tried to save you."

"Save me from what, Dad?" Larry implored, taking a step toward his father. "Just put down the gun, and tell me why you're doing this."

"Don't come any closer!" Stan commanded, pointing the gun at Mary once more.

"Okay, Dad," Larry said, raising his hands and backing off.

"None of you understand what I've had to go through! I have to do this for you, son!"

"I don't want this," Larry whimpered as he began to cry. "I just want my dad."

Stan let out an agonized wail and fell to his knees. Jenny rushed to her mother's side. Before Larry could react, Stan raised the gun once more.

"I'm sorry, son," he said. "It's finished."

"Drop the gun, Mr. Hirsch!" Jay yelled from somewhere behind him.

"Better yet, give me a reason to shoot you, motherfucker!" John shouted.

Stan's head dropped. For a moment Jenny held out hope that it was over. Then Stan looked up, and she saw the sorrow in his eyes. Jenny understood that, for him, this was an all-or-nothing mission. She didn't hate him at that moment. Instead, she pitied him, and she wept, for she knew that what followed would destroy the man she loved.

"I'm sorry, Billy," Stan said mournfully. "I love you."

Before anyone inside could react, Stan rose to his feet and turned toward Jay with his weapon raised. Larry shouted something, but Jenny couldn't focus on what it was. She reached out and gripped him tightly, holding him in place. Jenny buried her face in his chest as the shots rang out. Stan's limp, lifeless body collapsed onto the kitchen floor with a thud. The killer who had haunted Traders' Point was dead. It was finally over.

EPILOGUE

A couple of hours later, the scent of blood mixed with birthday cake brought me back to my senses. I was lying on the floor beside your mother's corpse, covered in her blood. Looking up, I saw that her face had been completely obliterated, and I threw up beside her. After several minutes of retching, I pulled myself to my feet and began to come to grips with what I had done. I had killed your mother, the woman I had professed to love. I was a monster, and I didn't think I could live with myself. I thought about killing myself, but then I heard you begin to cry.

I wish I had had the courage to call the police and turn myself in, but your mother had been right. I was a coward, and I depended on my father for everything. I went to the kitchen and made myself a stiff drink. Then I called my father. He told me to take you and leave the house. He said he would take care of everything. I naïvely believed that he meant he would make your mother disappear, much as he had her lover years before. At worst I thought he would contact the police and try to get me the best deal possible, so I listened to him. To this day I wish I hadn't.

The following morning your mother's brother was taken into custody. The police report claimed to find her blood all over his clothes and his fingerprints on the murder weapon. Your Uncle Maverick swore that he didn't do it, but his level of intoxication from the previous evening had left him with a total memory loss. Additionally, over the next few days, "evidence" and "witnesses" emerged to reveal incriminating details such as his "extreme jealousy" of his sister's success and details of his plot to take revenge on Marsha for forcing him to move into her place and work as a servant. Of course, all of this evidence was fabricated by my father.

I wanted desperately to speak up at the trial about what I knew, but I was sure that if I did I would be the one who faced a lifetime behind bars. As much as I deserved that fate, the thought of my father raising you as he had me was a far worse fate than you deserved. I realized you were all that mattered, and I knew I had to get you away from the rapist who had destroyed our family. I spent the next few months pretending that things had gone back to normal. In reality, I was siphoning money out of my family's company and preparing to leave for the farthest corner of the country to begin a new life with you. However, I knew that my father would never stop hunting us as long as he was free to do so.

Before I left town, I compiled enough evidence to set your Uncle Maverick free and place the blame for framing him squarely upon my father. I had hoped that the police would arrest him and that would give me time to make my escape. I didn't realize how dire this decision would be. I never imagined that my father would make bail the same day that Maverick was released from prison, pending a new trial. By the time I learned that he had killed and robbed your grandfather, we had begun our new lives here in Traders' Point.

I always feared the day would come when your Uncle Maverick found me and tried to complete his revenge. Although I deserve nothing more than his wrath, I can never let you learn the truth of our family. So long as there was still breath in my lungs, I would not allow you to be destroyed by the mistakes my father and I made. That's why I tried to kill your uncle and everyone he spoke to, to make sure that you did not learn the truth of how you came to be and how your mother really died.

If you're reading this letter, that means I have failed in this mission. Therefore, I wanted to make sure that I was the one to tell you the truth. No matter what you may think of me or of what my father did, know that you're my son, Billy, and I'll always love you. I just hope you can forgive me someday. I pray that you will not let the past change the wonderful man that you have become. Get married, son, have children, and find the life that I always wished for you to have.

Love,
Dad

Larry finished reading aloud the letter that he had found in father's pocket. The faces of those who listened ranged from somber to bitter.

Jenny pulled him into a fierce hug. "I love you," she whispered.

John spat on the ground. "Doesn't change what he did. My brother is still lying dead somewhere out there in the woods."

"I'll take you to his body," Mary said softly, taking his hand in hers. "You should know that he was a real hero. I wouldn't be alive were it not for him, and for you."

A tear fell down John's cheek. "He was always my hero."

They walked off toward the forest together. Jay reached out and shook Larry and Jenny's hands. "I hope there's no hard feelings," he said sheepishly.

"Turns out we were all wrong," Jenny replied with a smile. "Just as long as you let Kennedy out of his cell, I think we can call it square. I promised I would do what I could to set him free."

"I'll head over to the office right away," Jay replied, mirroring her smile. "Perhaps you can call the radio station and let everyone know that the danger has passed."

"Will do, Sheriff," Jenny stated.

They watched him walk off. Once Larry was sure they were alone, he turned to Jenny. "I wouldn't blame you if you wanted to break off our engagement. My dad did try to kill your mother, after all. Plus, I'm sure that, once everyone learns what he did, I won't be welcome to stay here."

"Nonsense!" Jenny exclaimed. "This is your home, Larry Hirsch, and we have a wedding to plan. Besides, I'm thinking a life as a shopkeeper might suit me just fine after all."

The sun rose over Traders' Point, sending a rainbow of elegant colours streaming across the sky. The October storms had finally passed, and the community knew peace once more.

ABOUT THE AUTHOR

A longtime fan of true crime shows and suspenseful thrillers, Jeremy Gernhaelder has been writing as a hobby since he was seven years old, even winning awards for his poetry during high school. While on stress leave from his job as a teacher in early 2020, he decided to elevate writing from a pastime to something he might pursue professionally. The result of that effort was the *Small Town Slashers* series, with *The Drifter* being the first installment. Jeremy was raised in the small town of Cayuga, Ontario, Canada. He currently lives in another small town, Lochaber, Quebec, with his fiancée, Anick Côté, their 4.5-year-old budgie, and their 3.5-year-old pug.

Milton Keynes UK
Ingram Content Group UK Ltd.
UKHW040950071123
432124UK00001B/96